PRAIRIE ATTACK!

"Fire!" Captain Cavanaugh ordered as the large Sioux war party thundered forward. He motioned to his trumpeter to be ready. After the Spencers had spat out four rounds each, he called to the bugler, "Sound charge!"

The bugle call echoed across the high prairie and the 110 cavalrymen surged forward, the outer ends of the long company front bending inward to surround the hostiles. Troopers reloaded their Spencers on the gallop, while others put away their long guns and drew their six guns to find targets at close range.

In the first volley of fire, two of the hostiles went down and two horses were hit, throwing their riders. The Indians galloped forward and to the side; a few even turned and retreated not liking the two-to-one odds. The mass of the two sides came together in a bloody melee of pistols firing, horses bellowing, and men dying. . . .

Other Books in the **ARROW & SABER** Series

OUSHATA MASSACRE

ARROW AND SABER

CAVANAUGH'S ISLAND
G.A. CARRINGTON

A DELL BOOK

Published by
Dell Publishing
a division of Bantam Doubleday Dell
Publishing Group, Inc.
666 Fifth Avenue
New York, New York 10103

ISBN: 0-440-20380-5

Printed in the United States of America
Published simultaneously in Canada

October 1989

10 9 8 7 6 5 4 3 2 1

KRI

Cavanaugh's Island

Chapter One

Major Andrew Owensby tracked the savage with his long gun and squeezed off a shot. He had led the charging Indian just right and the .52-caliber slug from the rifled bore of the Spencer carbine slammed through the redman's chest and jolted him off his charging war pony.

"Yeah, by damn!" Major Owensby muttered as he levered another round into the Spencer. He shifted his weapon to the other side of the broken-out window pane of the stage line's west Kansas swing station and fired again.

He swore and worked the lever, pumping a fresh round into the weapon, and found an attacker coming directly at him. Lifting his weapon, he fired in an instant due to long practice and a batch of natural instinct. The round hit the war-painted Indian, who was less than ten feet away, in the face, taking off half of the back of his skull. The war pony swerved around the small cabin with the dead Sioux warrior still on its back.

A rifle round caught the window frame near Major Owensby and sent splinters flying into the room.

"They gettin' a belly full!" a teamster firing from the window on the other side screeched. His name was Vern Tuttwise and he was the driver of the Butterfield Overland stage that had just pulled into the swing station for fresh horses when the Cheyenne raiding party hit. The Cheyenne had attacked without warning. "Sure as hell, they're getting tired of being shot up," Tuttwise said. "They'll be hauling their red asses out of here any minute now."

That was when the eight people barricaded in the small building smelled smoke.

"What kind of roof this thing got on it?" Major Owensby barked.

Vern Tuttwise looked up. "Shingles, and they're what's burning!"

Major Owensby glanced at the two women crouched beside the stone fireplace, the most secure spot in the one-room structure. They looked frightened but seemed to be holding up well. No damn tears at least.

A hardware drummer looked out the other window and snapped off a shot from his six-gun. "Get closer, you cowards!" the hardware salesman shouted.

Two stable hands and the shotgun guard took turns with rifles at the third window toward the front of the cabin. The guard had traded his scatter gun for a Springfield and used it with cool efficiency. "Jeeze, how many of them heathens are out there?" he asked. He tracked a hostile on his horse and fired. The slug cut into the horse's neck and it went down in a cloud of dust.

Major Owensby figured they had maybe ten minutes before smoke would come pouring in so thick they'd have to run for it — right into the arrows and bullets from the Cheyenne out there.

"How many Indians left?" Major Owensby demanded. He saw four out his window, three of them riding off the far side of their horses, giving a man no target.

"I got three over here," the driver said.

"Only two back here, and one's wounded," one of the stable hands said.

"No choice," Major Owensby said. "Aim for the horses. Without their mounts, these Cheyenne can't fight worth a damn!" He looked at the women. "Excuse the language, ladies. Now cut down those Indian ponies!"

The rattle of gunfire from the cabin erupted again. The younger woman, a blonde about twenty, held her hands over her ears. The older woman frowned at her, then looked up at the Army major waiting stoically.

Major Owensby cut down two war ponies before the Indians realized the new strategy. They quickly pulled back out of pistol range and behind a small rise. As they fled, the major could count the hostiles. They had only five horses left. He opened the front door, letting it bang against the wall, and a gush of fresh air came with it. No rifle fire came through.

He sprawled on his belly on the rough wood floor near the door and checked through the opening. Smoke filtered down through the sheeting on the roof.

The creek bed, he thought, had a four-foot bank. They had to get there before the fire got any worse. Smoke spread down now all the way to the floor and one of the women was coughing. Major Owensby's eyes began to smart. The riverbank was their only hope. He crawled over to Tuttwise.

"I'm going first with the ladies. You men cover us. Fire at the savages and keep them busy. Then the rest of you come in a bunch and I'll cover you. Head straight for the creek. Better than getting roasted alive in this shack." A weak place in the roof sagged in and they saw flames. A three-foot-long sheeting board from the roof fell through the burned-out rafters.

"Ladies, come up here, please," the major said gently. He slipped the sling on his Spencer over his shoulder and nodded at the women. They came quickly and huddled beside the door. He stood at the other side of the opening and jabbed a stubby finger at the teamster. "Time to start covering us, Tuttwise. Now!" he shouted, then took the women, one by each hand, and ran out the door. Turning a hard left, he raced for the creek and the lifesaving protection of the four-foot dropoff.

Three rounds came toward them but missed. They were out of range of arrows. He jumped down the bank first, then caught the youngest woman as she teetered and fell over. The older woman sat down and skidded to the bottom. He unslung his Spencer and began firing at the cluster of Indians a hundred yards off. As usual, there was no Indian commander, or leader telling the Indian warriors what to do; each was a strategist and a general to himself. That was why the Army would eventually

4

whip the redskin warriors into submission, Owensby assured himself.

Suddenly, he heard a war cry and two Cheyenne warriors galloped forward. The old army Indian fighter figured that both warriors would stop, wheel around and race away from the cabin. Owensby had seen the harassing tactic a dozen times before and tracked one rider through the sights of his Spencer. The minute the redskin stopped his horse to wheel it around, the major fired. When the .52-caliber slug hit the rider, it took a chunk of flesh off his middle, dumping him over his mount's neck.

Out of the corner of his eye, Owensby saw the five men from the cabin charging the creek. The major fired as quickly as he could lever the rounds in the Spencer carbine until it was empty.

He grabbed another tube of rounds from the Blakeslee Quickloader packet over his shoulder, yanked the empty tube out of the baseplate of the Spencer, and pushed in the new tube. He charged a round into the chamber with the cocking lever under the trigger and then fired again quickly. At a hundred yards it was like they were in the same room. He'd had this personal Spencer weapon sighted by experts. He could blow the wings off a horsefly at a hundred yards and never harm the body.

Major Owensby put down another horse, then the men from the cabin began jumping over the side of the bank and started firing as soon as they got in position.

"Anybody get hit?" Owensby demanded.

"Yes, sir," one of the stable hands called. "Caught an arrow in the leg early on, but I broke it off."

"Damn fine work, son. Just hold on a few more minutes. We got out of the cabin, but we're not safe yet. These bas" . . . he glanced at the women, "these Cheyenne will circle around and fire from the other side. We'll have to split up so half of us go across the creek to that other bank."

Three of the men lifted up and splashed across the ankle-deep water to the far bank twenty feet away and picked out firing positions.

The cabin burned fiercely now. They could feel the heat.

"There goes my last deck of cards," one of the stable hands said.

"Cards? I just lost a new pair of pants and my best boots," the other swing station worker said.

"How far from here to Fort Wallace?" the major asked.

The driver looked up. "Right on to ten miles," Tuttwise said. "We was to get fresh horses here, but the Cheyenne kind of spoiled that."

"No sense worrying about that now, here they come. Every rifle back on this side. You three, come back over here," the major bellowed. "Wait until you can see them good before we fire," he ordered. "Don't know about you boys, but I'm getting a mite short of rounds."

"I got six left," the driver said.

"Ten or so here," another man added.

The teamster had five. The two stable hands had ten each.

"Here they come," Major Owensby said. "They'll charge past yelling and screaming. Don't show yourselves except to fire, then drop down. Hit those horses and we'll have a chance."

The Cheyenne raced forward in a line, one after the other. Three men shot the first Indian off his horse and the others slanted away from the creek.

Another horse fell in the ragged firing that followed. Then they were past and into the brush near the creek below the burning cabin. A billowing tower of black smoke climbed into the Kansas sky as the rest of the roof fell in.

"They'll be back," Major Owensby said. He knew what came next. The Cheyenne would creep up on them through the brush and be within easy bow-and-arrow range. He figured they had one chance in six of getting out of this alive. Damn, one in six. And to think of all of the tight spots he had been in during the Civil War and since then fighting a dozen different Indian tribes.

"Don't worry, ladies," he said touching the brim of his non-regulation army hat with a small plume on it. "We've got them on the run. They'll be pulling out of here right quickly now."

Vern Tuttwise looked at him and scowled. The driver knew better. Still, why paint a bad picture for the women. They'd know soon enough. He still had his six-gun. If everyone went down, he would save three rounds, two for the women and one for himself.

Major Owensby checked the Cheyenne. They had circled behind some brush where the creek bent and were now out of sight. They would regroup and catch any loose war ponies. They'd be back.

If he had even half a troop of cavalry, he'd run those savages down and blast them right into hell. The major rubbed a weathered hand over his face, tanned and windburned from many campaigns in the field. No time for wishful thinking now. He'd had a good life. Didn't make permanent rank of light colonel, but he still had been a Brigadier General during the war. Had a whole damn division of infantry and artillery. Brevet, but what the hell? He might never get his star back now.

"Here they come," the hardware drummer called.

Six of them, all in a pack, thundered forward heading straight for the creek bed where the six men and two women huddled.

"Knock down the front ones," the major bellowed. "They'll try to overrun us!"

The Cheyenne were less than a hundred yards away and storming forward when Major Owensby heard a shot from the right. He looked that way and saw twenty horsemen at full gallop. The man in front had a guideon snapping in the breeze. The dark blue blouses and sky blue pants could only mean they were U.S. Cavalry.

The cavalrymen charged straight at the surprised Cheyenne. Army carbines barked as the platoon front of mounted men spurred toward the hostiles in an open charge so each man could fire. The Cheyenne broke off their attack, wheeled around, and galloped away from the onrushing Horse Soldiers.

"Be damned," Tuttwise said. "Looks like your escort came to fetch you, Major."

Half of the troopers continued to chase the hostiles, the rest swung off and raced up to the burning stage coach swing station. The mounted soldiers checked four dead Indians and three horses as they came forward, making sure the Cheyenne were only spirits now.

A tall cavalry Captain rode up to the riverbank and dismounted. He snapped a salute to the officer in uniform still leaning against the dirt bank. He was twenty-seven years old, over six feet tall, with blue eyes and brown hair. He had a "cavalry tan" and smiled at the officer in the creek bed.

"Major, Captain Marcus Cavanaugh, acting commander of Fort Wallace, at your service."

The major waved his right hand in a half salute and scowled.

"Damn glad to see you, Captain. We jumped out of the frying pan over there into a fire. Figure we had about an hour left. Help the ladies out of here."

Captain Cavanaugh jumped down the embankment, took the younger woman's hand, and helped her to stand, then led her up the bank. He came back for the older woman, who thanked him as she brushed the dirt off her long skirt.

The young captain returned to the major, who still leaned against the embankment. Cavanaugh was surprised at the man's appearance. The officer was short and squat, overweight, with a scraggly beard that would never pass inspection. Beards were supposed to be kept "neat and short," according to the new regulations. His uniform was the strangest combination of officer's clothing Cavanaugh had ever seen. His shell jacket had a double row of buttons with a floppy sailor-type collar and knotted kerchief. The lower sleeves of the shell jacket were festooned with bright red gallons of embroidery with metallic threads, much as the Confederate officers used to show rank. His civilian dark blue trousers were store bought and his boots were polished leather that came ten inches above his knees.

The major jumped quickly up the embankment, surprising Captain Cavanaugh with his agility. "Well now, what do we have left here?" Major Owensby asked, looking around.

The stage was intact, but the lead horse was down in the traces. The stable hands quickly ran and unhitched the animal and put it out of its misery with a pistol shot. Then they turned the stage sharply and drove the rig away from the dead horse. They harnessed a new lead horse in its place.

"Looks like you've got a cavalry escort into Pond Creek Station, if that's all right with the major."

"Fine by me. But tell me, Cavanaugh, how you came to be around this part of the trail."

Captain Cavanaugh gave a quiet order to a sergeant, then turned back to the major.

"Out on a training patrol, sir. Actually, checking to see how well the men are progressing. We received thirty new troopers last month with no training at all, as usual. Sir, I'd guess that you're Major Owensby, the new commander of Fort Wallace, home of the Thirteenth Cavalry Regiment. Welcome, sir."

The major looked at the captain and nodded. "Right, I'm the one, if we ever get there. Tuttwise, when do we leave this place?" he yelled at the driver.

"A few minutes, Major. I want to check the other horses."

The major looked back. "What's your TO & E strength, Cavanaugh?"

"We're assigned twelve troops of cavalry. Right now we have an average of one officer per troop instead of three, and two sergeants instead of five per troop. Instead of seventy-two privates we average about forty. Probably about the same as it is all over the army."

"Sounds familiar. Do more with fewer men and fewer dollars. I've been through that." His small black eyes seemed to stare right through the Captain. The major's face twisted a minute in frustration. "Wanted to tell you, Captain, that I didn't ask

10

for this post . . . but you know the Army. Go where we're goddamned well sent." They walked over to the stage. "What about the headquarters staff?"

"About the same, sir. We're short about forty percent of our officer TO & E, but we're almost up to strength on our enlisted specialists."

"That sounds normal, too. Captain, I'm curious. How did you know that we were in trouble over here?"

"One of my outriders said he heard rifle fire, so we headed this way. We were about two miles off. Then we saw smoke and came at a gallop."

The old soldier took off his hat, revealing thinning brown hair, and wiped the sweat off his forehead. "Captain, you got here at the right time. We might have held them off one more charge, but I'm not sure. My troops were damn thin and we had less than five rounds per man. Damn glad you showed up."

"Our pleasure, Captain. Most of these men had never seen a hostile. Good for them to get a shot at the enemy for the first time." He grinned. "Besides," Captain Cavanaugh cleared his throat, "there's a pretty young lady in your group. Now, sir, let me provide you a mount for the trip back."

The major waved his hand. "I'll stick to the stage. I'm not as good on a horse as I used to be. I'm sore enough from bouncing around in this infernal machine they call a stagecoach."

"Everyone on board, sir," Tuttwise said. "We'll be heading out now. One of the stable hands will ride in with us on a mount. Damned hostiles killed four of our remuda, so Art has to get some replacement animals."

The two women were already on board. The troopers had caught two of the Indian ponies, and they would be taken back to the fort along with an assortment of short bows, arrows, and the quivers that had laced the backs of the hostiles.

After they mounted up, Tuttwise waved at the other stable hand and told him to hide in the brush until Art got back. Then Tuttwise cracked the whip and the horses moved forward. It took a while for the new lead mare to work into the rhythm already established by the other horses. It would be a slow trip to the next stop.

Captain Cavanaugh put two outriders on both sides of the stage road. The first rode a quarter of a mile out and the second another quarter of a mile. They would report any sighting of hostiles or other problems. He moved to the front of the stage, judged the speed, then took ten troopers as a lead escort, leaving the rest of the men under Sergeant York to bring up the rear guard.

The tired horses slowed steadily, and Tuttwise dropped them to a walk for the last mile.

"Ain't aiming to pay for any horse that I put down 'cause of the way I drive," Tuttwise explained to Captain Cavanaugh when the captain came back to check on why the rig was moving forward at a walk. "That second lead bay up there is about ready to go down. Would have if I'd even trotted her for another mile. We got time. Hell, I figure I've got another thirty years at least. What difference is a half hour going to make?"

· They pulled into Pond Creek Station three hours late. This was a fifty-mile station, and here the driver would change and the passengers could have something to eat at a family-style table.

An army ambulance waited at the station. First Lieutenant Winchester saluted smartly after failing to mask his surprise at the appearance of his new fort commander.

"Lieutenant Winchester, sir. Welcome to Fort Wallace. I have a rig here to drive you the final mile out to the fort."

"Good, Lieutenant. Better than walking. You have any kin in the Army? I used to know a Colonel Winchester. We called him Winnie . . . Yep, he was Harold Winchester. Infantry."

"That was my uncle, sir. He was killed in the war."

"That right? Hell, he was a good man. Never any complaints when Winnie was on the job. Let's get moving, Lieutenant. I could use a good hot bath and some fresh clothes."

Lieutenant Winchester led the major to the army ambulance. There was no provision made for moving personnel by vehicle in the Army. The regulation army ambulance was the best sprung and was often used to transport officers and their families from one post to another.

As Owensby climbed into the ambulance, his luggage was quickly taken out of the rear boot of the stage and stowed on board the wagon. Cavanaugh and Winchester mounted up and led the wagon, along with an honor guard of ten mounted troopers, south toward Fort Wallace.

"What in hell kind of a major is Owensby? When the men see their new commander dressed out of reg, we can kiss discipline good-bye."

"Next time I see Colonel Custer, I'll ask him what he thinks about non-regulation officer uniforms."

Lieutenant Winchester frowned and they rode for the fort.

Chapter Two

Struggling to keep up with his partner, Byron Foster rode doggedly onward on his big sorrel stallion. The horse was a beauty, taller than most range horses and reddish-brown in color with an almost pure white mane and tail. He had once refused an offer of $300 for "Big Mike," as he called him.

Foster himself was no beauty. The five-foot three-inch tall man was nearly square, fifty pounds overweight, and riding a horse was not his favorite way to travel long distances. His face was soft and pale, with small blue eyes hidden behind folds and puckers of flesh. His nose had been broken and spread out to twice its normal size in his early days as a saloon brawler. Now he was settled down as the sutler at Fort Wallace.

Since 1867, the official term for the commercial merchant establishment that supplied each fort was "trader's store," but most troopers and civilians still called it by its original name of sutler's store.

Foster's sorrel moved at a fast walk now through a small valley along a creek that would dump into the Arikaree River. The Arikaree was the central fork of the Republican River that wound into Nebraska, then back into central Kansas. The two riders had crossed the Kansas state line and were now in eastern Colorado Territory, some eighty-five miles northwest of Fort Wallace.

"Where'n hell is this place you found, Gates? My ass ain't got the callouses yours got," Foster called to the man riding just in front of him.

"Just hold to your leather, tenderfoot. Maybe I should have picked myself a better partner. Damn, you've been bellyaching half the time since we left Wallace two days ago."

"Told you I ain't no cavalry rider," Foster spat back in self-defense.

Toby Gates grinned and moved ahead on his dark gray dun mare. Gates looked about forty, but he was only twenty-eight. Fast, hard living had taken its toll. He had been a gambler on the Mississippi but wasn't good enough at poker or cheating to last long there.

At five-ten, he was slate thin, looking like he could slip right through the steel tines of a pitchfork. He had watery green eyes, a drooping mouth, and high cheekbones that left his cheeks hollow and sunken. His hair was shoulder length because he hated barber shops; he whacked it off with a pair of sheep shears when he figured it was too long. The Indians liked to see his long hair. His hands were nervous, always moving.

Now he had a United States license to do trading with the friendly tribes — if he could find any. He knew some of the Sioux tongue and a little of Cheyenne. Most tribes tolerated him because he brought them knives and steel, which they could use to make lance tips with and arrowheads. By law he was prevented from selling the Indians any guns, rifles, gunpowder, or lead shot, but he did just fine with knives and axes.

"All I know is that you better be right about that gold."

"Damn your hide, Foster, I told you I'm sure as hell that there's gold there. Hell, I been in gold strikes before. Was even in California at some of the lodes out there. I know the signs, and they sure as shooting are along that creek. The upthrust fronts this bluff. But it ain't worn down. It's a damn solid slab that I bet come from about ten miles down. Got to be gold in that slab. Fact is, I saw a glint shining big as you please and would've pinched a chunk for the appraiser if those Cheyenne weren't camped there."

"Hope to God you can find that same spot again."

"Shut up and smile," Gates shot back. "I'm the guy who's gonna make you rich."

"Hell, I don't mind getting rich, I just don't want to wind up getting scalped out here by your friendly Sioux cutthroats. Partnership ain't worth nothing if'n you're dead."

Gates shook his head and urged his mare forward.

A half mile later they came to some heavy brush along the banks of the Arikaree. They edged out slowly and checked for hostiles, but the big valley was empty. They saw no smoke, smelled none, and could see no tepees along the shallow river. The water flow here was about fifty yards across, but not more than ankle deep anyplace. In some spots islands showed and in others the water lay still in pools.

They turned sharply to the right and moved along the edge of the valley for a quarter of a mile through an open area, then turned right again up a tributary and toward a suddenly steep grade and a towering granite bluff.

The rock tower rose more than a hundred feet without a crack or shelf or rock fall. It looked like a smooth slab of rock in one single, giant piece.

They rode to the base of the slab, where the gentle waters of the tiny creek flowed past it. Gates got off his horse and stretched.

"Here's your gold mine, partner. How does it look?" Gates asked.

"Looks like a perfect spot to get a good drink and rest my ass," Foster said, stepping down gingerly.

"Look at that! An upthrust, pure and simple. There's got to be gold around here somewhere. This one came up from way down deep and had to drag some gold and silver along with it."

"So show me, big talker," Foster spat.

Gates dug into his saddlebag and took a rock hammer, a hatchetlike tool with a square hammer head on one side and a steel pick blade on the other. He walked through the shallow water and began hitting the upthrust with the pick end of the tool. It rang out strong and solid.

He worked around to the dry land and a little farther into some low brush to the left. Gates mumbled to himself, hit the rock a few more times, then was quiet. He worked around the huge solid base

18

slowly and a half hour later came back and sat down near Foster and shook his head.

"Nothing so far. Still got the other half to work. I'd make you help but you don't know what to look for." He had a drink, got up and went to the other side and began pushing down brush and examining the rock. It was a half hour later and dusk was falling when the man yelled out.

"Oh, damn!" Gates screeched. "Oh, damn! Foster, get your butt over here! Come see what I found!"

Foster stepped through the shallows and pushed back the brush. "So, what's so important?"

Near the bottom of the huge slab there was another ledge of rock that had cracks and weathering places where water had seeped in, frozen, and cracked it. Now, Gates had expanded the crack and broken off a wide slab of the rock. Behind it glowed a three-inch streak of what looked like solid gold.

"Sweet mother!" Foster whispered. "Is it . . . is that gold?"

"Never seen it like that before, but it's got to be." He hit the streak with his pick and the end sunk into the soft substance.

"Break off some of it so we can get it assayed," the sutler yelped. "Christ, looks like damn near pure gold!"

Gates knelt there and stared at the rock. "What . . . " he stopped and swallowed hard. "What if this whole damn upthrust has a gold center! That's enough gold to make us millionaires!"

"Break some off!" Foster shouted.

"First, we hide the horses, just in case some Indians show up here ready to set up camp again. I'd as soon not try to explain why I rode up here without a pack horse and no goods to sell."

They moved the horses to the side of the monolith in some heavy brush and tied them, then took rifles and a canvas bag and went back to their discovery.

It was dusk now and they'd have only another five minutes of light. Furiously, Gates whaled at the rock and at last broke off some chunks of the granite with the gold on the side. He gouged out some of the solid gold as well and dropped the samples in the sack.

"Want me to make a torch so you can see what the hell you're doing?" Foster asked.

Gates snorted. "Sure, and let every Indian within five miles know we're here? Hell, no. We bed down for the night and finish getting our samples in the morning. Then we fix up this spot so it looks like nobody has ever even walked through here. Remember that. A white man's got to be damned double careful in Indian country if he wants to keep his scalp."

They rolled out their blankets deep in the protecting brush, and chewed on jerky and some dried fruit for their supper.

"That's really gold, Gates. You wouldn't go and try to fool me," Foster said with his mouth full.

"If that's not gold, you can have my horse tomorrow," Gates said. "Now we got ourselves a damn big problem. This is still Indian country. The bastards run all over here whenever they want to, Cheyenne, Sioux, and lots of Arapaho. I've sold to them all. But they won't ever let us dig out this gold. What we gonna do, hire ourselves an army to get in here and work our mine, hoping that we can stay alive?"

"I ain't got that kind of money," Foster said as he tried to find a comfortable position on the hard ground.

"Who has any money? Anyway, we couldn't hire enough men. The damned redskins must have near a thousand warriors in this area, all the tribes. Hell, we'd be slaughtered."

"Maybe we could come in when the tribes go to their winter camps?" Foster suggested.

"Yeah, might. Trouble is, I've seen six or eight bands use the Arikaree for their winter camp. They probably will again, soon as their fall hunt is over."

Foster growled, "Christ, you mean we know where this gold is and we can't do a damn thing about getting it out and selling it?"

"Sounds about right. We need some idea to change the situation."

"We could wait until settlers move into the valley and chase out the Indians."

"Be old men by then."

Foster chuckled. "Hey, the Army. We can sic the Army on the bastards and chase their asses right out of here."

Gates sighed. "Yeah, they might be able to do it, but nobody tells the Army what to do. You know that from working with them. Be years before the Army gets the Sioux pushed out of this corner of Colorado Territory."

Foster turned over on his stomach and propped his chin in his hands. "That's it then, I reckon."

"We think on it until morning. Maybe we'll get an idea. If not, we dig out as much of the gold as we can and get back to civilization."

"Without getting scalped, of course," Foster added. They both thought about their problem as they drifted off to sleep.

Gates had been up for an hour when Byron Foster woke up the next morning. He was sore and stiff and grouchy. He sat up and rubbed his eyes, then took some of the jerky and dried fruit that Gates gave him.

"Why the hell did I ever let you talk me into this?" Foster growled.

"Because you want to get rich, too, just like me. I checked down the Arikaree. Not a sign of a redskin out there. Let's dig off some more of that gold and get out of here while we can."

For two hours they took turns digging into the gold vein and the harder rock around it, then figured they had about fifty pounds of the gold ore and pure gold in their canvas sack. They tied it on the back of Foster's horse because it was stronger and started down the tributary to the Arikaree and back toward Wallace.

Toby Gates led the pair and worked slowly toward the edge of the brush so he could see down the main valley.

"Oh, damn!" Gates said, stopping suddenly. "We got company. A band of Cheyenne by the looks, moving in from the other end of the valley. Usual long line of horses and travois. Just coming in. If we stick to the brush along here we should be able to slip out before they get this far upstream."

" *Should* be able to, Gates? What happens if we don't?"

"Target practice, I'd say, and we're the targets." He moved his dun to the left through more brush and away from the nearing band of Cheyenne. They worked through the brush for nearly half an hour, moving slowly upstream toward the tributary that would lead them southeast into the range of hills and away from the Cheyenne.

Then the brush ended. There was nothing but a half mile of open meadow in front of them and the creek upstream that would be their highway out of the valley.

They sat their horses at the edge of the brush, looking at the open space. Before they could comment, two warriors on ponies came galloping along the river heading upstream, directly through the area they had to cross.

"Well, damn!" Toby Gates said. He turned back into the brush and headed up the slope toward a ridgeline that was covered with trees. "Hope that critter of yours is good at climbing hills, cause with Cheyenne all over the valley, that's the only way we're getting out of here alive."

They worked slowly up the steep slopes, cutting back and forth in a zigzag trail to get to the top. The trees and brush were thick and it took them longer to make it than Gates had figured. Once over the first ridge, they struck out to the southeast and moved quicker.

"Made it, by damn!" Gates said after reaching the second ridge. "Now all we have to do is ride back to Wallace."

That night around the campfire, they talked about their problem again. It was a stumper. Then Gates put another stick on the small fire and grinned.

"Hell, we can help convince the Army it should swing up through the Arikaree valley," Gates said. "I got just the idea how to do it. We get the Indians so riled up, they start hitting every white eye they find.

Then the Army will have to push in there and clean them out. Hell, it's their job to protect us innocent civilians."

"No way to stir up the Indians without getting killed ourselves. I gave up on our gold mine about the time we spotted them Cheyenne this morning."

"Leave it up to me. I'll do it, and you don't even have to know about it."

"Suits me. You got sneaky ways, Toby Gates. I'll be partners with you in that strike, but I don't want in on none of the sneaky stuff to get us there."

"Deal," Gates said, shaking hands with Foster.

He knew exactly how he was going to do it. For the past year he'd known a young man in town by the name of Willy Hedbetter. A hardworking man of about thirty who had an instant flash temper.

Willy often said if any savage ever hurt him or his family, he'd take off on a campaign to shoot up every damn Indian he could find. He spelled it out one night over some beers. Said he had an old Big Fifty, a Sharps .50-100 his uncle had used to kill buffalo. He could shoot Indians from half a mile away with that gun.

Gates remembered that Willy had a brother who lived on a small ranch about ten miles out of town. Now if some Cheyennes hit that ranch and massacred everyone, it surely would set Willy off on his killing spree in retaliation. Indians would be madder than hell and start killing settlers, starting a bona fide territory war.

And the troops at Fort Wallace would likely finish it.

Chapter Three

When the army Rucker ambulance wagon rolled up to Fort Wallace, Kansas, there was no parade ready to greet the new commander. He was over three hours late and the small honor guard that had been ready had long since been dismissed.

The ambulance drove past the first building and the parade grounds up to the fort's commanding officer's headquarters. Lieutenant Winchester was there, dismounted and ready to help the commander step down from the ambulance.

"Sir, I'm sorry we have no parade ready for you. I'll see to it that we have a formal parade and a proper change-of-command ceremony tomorrow at noon."

"Won't be necessary, Lieutenant. I don't hold much to all that spit and polish. We're here to get a job done, not put on a damn show. The only change-of-command whoopteedo I want is to get into my quarters and take a bath."

"Yes, sir, Major Owensby. Your quarters are down this way, second door. I'm sure it's been cleaned for you and should be ready. We've assigned Corporal Rogers as orderly until you pick out your own. He's been told to have hot water ready. Your orderly is a fine cook as well, sir, and he has a stocked larder. If you want . . . "

Major Owensby waved his hand. "I know the drill, Lieutenant. I've been in the Army long enough. That will be all."

The major marched to the open door of his quarters and took the salute from Corporal Rogers. The major went inside, waved a half salute at the corporal, and closed the door. He looked at the neatly dressed trooper.

"Rogers, is it?"

"Yes, sir."

"Fine. You're saddled with me for a few days, until you decide whether or not you want the job. I'm not a hard man to work for. Most enlisted men get a raw deal in the Army. You won't. I don't stand on ceremony. Just do your job and we'll get on fine. You'll eat here, bunk in one of the rooms if you want to. That way you'll be free of the damn sergeants. Now, how's the hot water coming?"

Captain Marcus Cavanaugh turned his mount over to his orderly at the regimental headquarters and walked inside. First Lieutenant Ike Jackman looked up from the morning report, his round face full of questions.

"So? So, what's he like?" Ike asked.

Marcus stopped and laughed. "Not Winchester's type of officer. Not a ramrod regulations officer. I'd say we don't have to worry about a formal parade every Saturday. They get everything of mine cleaned out of the commander's office?"

"Sure did, Captain. Your orderly did the last of it. All back in your office next door. We set up the major for things he'll need right away."

Lieutenant Jackman was a cherub of a man, medium sized with a broad face, brown eyes, and brown hair with just a touch of a dark beard showing and a full brown moustache. He dressed precisely correct with the proper uniform, which was always laundered and pressed. His laundry was done twice a week instead of once and he did his own cooking. The officer's quarters he used were usually assigned to one of the majors slots in the regimental headquarters staff, but since there had been no majors at the fort, he was safe from getting ranked out of the three-bedroom house.

Jackman was West Point, twenty-eight years old and looking for a wife, but there were no prospects in the entire area. He was a good man at waiting and took care of the detail work as regimental adjutant with dedicated efficiency.

Marcus headed for his old office, where the executive officer of the regiment sat.

"Sir, what about that parade we had planned for the changing-of -command ceremony?" Lieutenant Jackman asked.

Marcus chuckled. "Don't reckon we'll have to worry about that. The major and I had a handshake just after he had an argument with fifteen Cheyenne out at the first swing station. I'd say the command has already changed." Marcus paused. "You put an orderly in his quarters?"

"Yes, sir. Rogers. Filled the supplies closet with the best we have." Jackman looked worried. "Some. Cheyenne attacked the major?"

"Hit the swing station about ten miles out east as the stage was about to change horses. They burned down the cabin, shot some horses. But the major led the passengers and crew into the creek bed and was fighting them off when our training patrol saw the smoke and galloped into the rescue."

"Just like in the western dime novels," Lieutenant Jackman said, grinning. "At least the major didn't get wounded. Then you escorted the stage into town?"

"About the size of it. It tells better than it happened."

"Maybe some day I'll get back out into the field."

"Maybe, but only when you get a replacement for yourself who can do your job better. Send for Sergeant York from that special training troop we set up. We need to talk."

"Yes, sir, Captain."

A private who had been sitting on a bench along the far side of the room stood and walked over to Lieutenant Jackman and nodded. He left by the front door.

Lieutenant Winchester came in, took off his black campaign hat with the wide brim and held it under his arm. He came to attention in front of the adjutant.

"Sir, Lieutenant Winchester to see Captain Cavanaugh."

"Winchester for . . . " Jackman shook his head. "Knock on the door and go on in. We're all friends here."

"Yes, but . . . "

"This isn't division headquarters or the Point. Just go on inside."

He knocked, then opened Captain Cavanaugh's door. "Sir, do you have a minute to talk?"

"Sure."

"I don't think we're going to have a parade for the major."

"I heard."

"And no changing-of-command ceremony."

"Yes, it seems that way."

Winchester squared his shoulders. "I respectfully suggest that it doesn't seem right to disregard basic command regulations."

"I remember once back at the Point," Cavanaugh began, staring up at the lieutenant, "when you were a class ahead of me and you picked me out as your target for special harassment for almost a year. Do you remember?"

"Yes, sir."

"That was part of your job — to whip the first-year men into shape. And you did damn fine. But in the field, there's no call to be knocking your men out over rule. Especially since it looks to me like Major Owensby plans to run the fort without much fanfare."

A knock sounded on the door, it opened, and Sergeant York came in.

"Trooper, we're busy here!" Winchester barked.

Sergeant York began to back out.

"Come on in, York. We were just about finished. You and I have some work to do on those recruits.

Have you asked Lieutenant Winchester to lead one of our training patrols?"

"No, sir, not yet, Captain."

"Good, I'll do it. Thursday morning, Winchester. We'll be doing a thirty-mile ride on scout to give the new men some training before they get into a fight and get butchered. Don't you think that's a good idea?"

"Yes, but . . . "

"Good, we'll see you there. Boots and saddles at six-fifteen."

"My company drill . . . "

"Lieutenant O'Hara can take care of that nicely. We'll count on your help. That's all, Lieutenant."

Winchester stormed out of the room, but closed the door gently.

Sergeant Lamar York grinned broadly as he held out the clipboard for Captain Cavanaugh to inspect.

"What are you grinning about, Sergeant."

"Was I grinning, sir? Just remembering a good joke, I reckon."

"I reckon you did, too. Now, how are your charges coming along?"

"Damn slow, sir. They need more riding training. Some of them can't even shoot their weapons. I'd say rifle training and target practice are the two biggest things. This afternoon the ones who fired didn't hit a single Indian. There were six up there, maybe 300 yards, and the men missed them all."

"Tomorrow, rifle practice. Field stripping their weapons, and prone and sitting positions target practice. Take care of it, Sergeant. Fifty rounds per man. Draw it from my supply with Sergeant Quinn over at the Quartermaster's office."

"Yes, sir."

"Keep after them, York. What you're doing is helping these men to save their own lives, and just maybe helping us to win a skirmish with the hostiles."

"Yes, sir. We've both been in enough to know about that." He saluted smartly, took Marcus' return salute, did an about face and walked out the door.

About half an hour later, Major Owensby walked in unannounced, his hair still wet from his bath.

"Don't get up, Cavanaugh. Need a favor. Can you walk me around this place? I want to find out what I've got to work with here besides half a roster."

"Be glad to, Major. As you said, about average on manpower strength. Damn good surgeon and an apprentice surgeon who just came in under Dr. Lassiter to learn the trade."

For the next two hours, the two men walked the fort, nosed into most of the buildings, checked the stables and the horses. The major had a long talk with Sergeant Udall, the veterinarian sergeant in charge.

As the shadows started to lengthen, they completed the tour, and the short, square commander pulled at his scraggly beard.

"Cavanaugh, I like the way you deal with people. Figure you can give me an honest rundown on the officers?"

"Figure I can, Major Owensby."

"Then come have supper with me. Rogers is fixing for three, so there should be plenty. As you can tell, I don't mind a good meal now and again. I want the lowdown on every officer on post. I'll remember it. Winchester I know enough about already — damn near too much. Let's start with the headquarters staff and then hit the troops. Hear we've got only one officer in most of our line troops."

They went to the commander's quarters, where Corporal Rogers had a fried chicken dinner with mashed potatoes, chicken gravy, fresh peas and carrots, and hot biscuits and jam and lots of hot coffee.

During the meal, Captain Cavanaugh gave his honest opinion and evaluation of every officer on the post. Now and then the major had a question, but mostly he listened.

When Cavanaugh came to Lieutenant Timothy O'Hara, the major held up his fork.

"Is there any problem with the lieutenant having his enlisted father on the same post? I heard about it only the day before I left Chicago."

"Lieutenant O'Hara has been on post for about six months now and we haven't had any problems that I've heard of. And I hear about most everything that goes on. He's sharp, well trained, went to the Point, and knows where his duty lies. Sergeant Major Kevin O'Hara is an excellent man and does a damn fine job. He's honest, fair, a good organizer, gets along well with the men. The only officer who seems to resent that his father is enlisted is Lieutenant Winchester."

"And they're both in A troop, right?"

"Yes, sir."

"Seems fine to me. Would you object to a glass of wine to polish off this fine meal, Captain?"

The next morning Major Owensby called Captain Cavanaugh into his office. His frown was a mile wide.

"What's this I hear about a dinner dance reception to be held in my honor tonight?"

32

Marcus shrugged. "Bound to happen, Major. You know how these army wives are."

"Your wife cook this thing up?" the major asked.

"No, I'm not married, sir. It's Major Lassiter, our chief surgeon. His wife Rebecca likes to organize these things. Seems to be good for morale."

"I see. Well, hell, I guess it can't be helped. At least I can meet all of my officers. Get that out of the way. Figured you might be able to stop the fool thing."

"Not when Rebecca has her mind made up."

"Yes, I guess we better go. My wife is back in Chicago. She said this was the end of the world and didn't want to come out here. I'm just as glad. Damn shame when they let women come on an army base, anyway. We have laundry women here?"

"Yes, sir. Mostly enlisted wives do that duty."

"Many whores?"

"Two for the officers, and as I remember, about fifteen work the enlisted."

"Yeah. I guess I can't change the system. I don't like it, never have, but it's better than what General Hooker tried. What the hell, I won't worry about it. Just so the whores don't cause any trouble."

"Been quiet lately, sir."

"Good."

"Major," Captain Cavanaugh began, changing the subject, "I'd like to put in a requisition for twenty thousand rounds of .52-caliber ammunition for the Spencer carbines. I'm working on a regiment-wide target practice system. Some of these recruits have never fired a weapon in their lives. We can call most of it ammunition fired in patrols and engagements with the hostiles."

"Think target practice does any good, Captain? Some of the brass back in Chicago have been stopping target practice."

"Yes, sir. But they don't have to lead men into the field who can't hit the side of the barracks if they're standing six feet away from the boards."

Major Owensky shook his head. "You've got a point. I'd have given a lot to have a squad of sharpshooters with me yesterday afternoon."

"Yes, sir. If our men can hit what they need to, instead of just firing blindly and hoping, we'll win more than we lose."

"Put in the requisition, I'll send it right to General Sheridan."

"Thank you, sir."

That night at the dinner, Rebecca Lassiter went all out. She was a big woman, nearly five-eight with a full figure and an infectious laugh. She should have been a diplomat. There never was a stranger in her home. She was a friend to all and had a small sweet face that automatically brought a smile from people meeting her for the first time.

The Lassiters had rolled up the carpet in the living room and put in a long table and benches for the supper. She served thirty-seven, including the wives of twelve officers.

The meal was delicious — ham, turkey and wild pheasant, half a dozen vegetables and side dishes, and three kinds of salad. For dessert she had found strawberries somewhere and fixed them on individual shortcakes with fresh whipped cream that everyone raved about.

After dinner, the men carried out the table and benches and four enlisted men came in to play for the dancing. One on piano, a fiddler, a guitar man, and the fourth on accordion. Before the dancing began there was a formal reception of the new commander and a receiving line. Captain Cavanaugh saw the major holding himself in check a time or two as he struggled through the formalities. When the last officer and lady had come through the line, Mrs. Lassiter called for the music and took the major by the hand.

"Since your lovely wife is in Chicago, I'll fill in for the first dance with our honored guest," she said. She swung the shorter, rotund officer onto the floor and proceeded to lead through the entire three minute dance. When it was over, Major Owensby headed for the punch bowl and took half a glass of the fruit juice punch and filled the rest of the cup from a flask of whiskey in his jacket pocket.

After the major had fortified himself, he danced with three of the younger and prettier women, then held court at a small table in the corner of the room and talked soldiering with Captain Cavanaugh, young Lieutenant O'Hara, and Major Lassiter, the surgeon and host.

As was the custom, none of the guests could leave until the honored guest did. Major Owensby took pity on himself and the other men and bowed out relatively early. Most of the couples stayed and danced until after one A.M.

Chapter Four

The next morning, Lieutenant O'Hara was waiting for Captain Cavanaugh when he came into his office just after breakfast. The captain invited him in and the young officer stood rigidly in front of his desk.

"Sir, Lieutenant Timothy O'Hara of Able Troop, Thirteenth Regiment. I respectfully request a change of duty assignment to another troop on this post."

Captain Cavanaugh looked at Lieutenant O'Hara with surprise. "What was that again, O'Hara?"

"I want out of Troop A and into another troop, sir!"

Captain Cavanaugh checked the officer closely. He was not a large man, five-nine perhaps, 140 pounds but strongly built with good shoulders and a trim waist. He was single, came out of his West Point class in the eighth spot out of forty-five, four higher than Cavanaugh had five years previous to his posting in the West. He had brownish-red hair and a full bushy moustache but otherwise clean-shaven. His green eyes were angry now.

"Sit down and relax, Lieutenant," Cavanaugh said, waving his hand. "Now tell me what this is all about."

Lieutenant O'Hara remained standing at attention in front of the desk. "I'd rather stand, sir. My reasons concern the unprofessional conduct of another officer whose name I'm prevented from stating out of military courtesy."

"Lieutenant O'Hara, I need you in Able Troop. I've made it our Quick Ride. We need two officers there for the best tactical operation of your fifty-one men."

"I know that, Captain. I hate to leave the men, but my position at present is intolerable and interferes with the performance of my duties."

"I respect your adherence to the honor code, O'Hara. I'll look into the problem. Give me a week. For now, just stay with your men."

"Thank you, sir. I don't mean to complain . . . "

"I'm glad you came in. Dismissed."

O'Hara returned Cavanaugh's salute, turned sharply and walked out.

The fort's executive officer dug into his paperwork and was halfway through with an overview of a request he was making for additional, vitally needed officers at Fort Wallace, when Jackman knocked and burst into the room.

"Sir. We just brought in a wounded civilian from an Indian raid. Major wants you over to Doc Lassiter's office right away."

Cavanaugh quickly caught up his three-inch leather belt with the holster attached which held his regulation revolver, and hurried out the office door. He trotted across the parade grounds to the medical office and sick bay.

Upon his arrival, he found Major Owensby questioning a civilian who had an arrow in his thigh and a bullet wound in his shoulder.

"You say they jumped you just at dawn. About a dozen warriors. What tribe?"

"Don't know, Major. They was all over us. I played dead after the first charge, then got behind the barn and ran into the trees along the creek. Martha, my wife, had been out that way on her little mare looking for some wild onions to transplant into our garden. I found her and we hid until the heathens left. They burned the house, barn, and shed to the ground and busted up the corral. My three range hands are dead and the Indians ran off with about forty head of horses and a herd of forty or fifty steers. I'm wiped out."

"What direction did they go when they left?" Captain Cavanaugh asked.

"Direction?" The rancher winced as doctor began to work on the arrow. "North."

"Major Owensby," Marcus Cavanaugh said sharply. "I request permission to take Able Troop in pursuit. Four days' rations. We can ride in forty-five minutes."

"Granted. You've got a good chance to run them down. They can't move fast with all that livestock."

The captain ran out of the medical office and directly to the Able Troop orderly room. Lieutenant O'Hara was there, and he took the order and barked it to his first sergeant.

It was exactly an hour later when Able Troop, with four Crow Indian scouts and Captain Cavanaugh, formed up on the parade ground and rode out past the Thirteenth Regimental headquarters building to the north.

Lieutenant Winchester led the unit, with Captain Cavanaugh and Lieutenant O'Hara behind him. As they assembled, the captain gave command over to Winchester, charging him to pursue, catch, and punish the attackers and recover the stolen livestock if possible. He would ride along as an observer.

They moved out of the fort at a six-mile-an-hour canter, and following the map drawn by the rancher found the burned out buildings eight miles north and west of the fort. Two of the Crow scouts had ridden ahead to the ranch when they spotted the still -smoking timbers on the barn and circled the place to pick up the tracks of the raiders.

Eagle Feather, the best Crow tracker on the post, came back and reported in broken English that there was a broad trail heading northwest, many horses, many beef, and twelve to fifteen Indian ponies.

It was just before midday when they headed along the Indian trail.

"Let's lift the pace," Captain Cavanaugh suggested to Lieutenant Winchester. "If we don't, we won't catch them before dark and they'll be gone for good."

Winchester agreed and gave the order. They moved the mounted line of cavalry into a lope that would eat up the distance between them and the savages while being as easy a gait for the horses as walking. The troopers were stretched out four abreast behind their officers, with the top sergeant bringing up the rear.

The scouts rode out ahead in a leapfrogging system. One galloped out a quarter of a mile to make sure of the trail and waited. The scout behind him rode to the lead scout, then a quarter of a mile beyond him, checking the trail. Then he stopped, and the first scout caught up and rode ahead. They could ride hard and still follow the trail using this system.

In this prairie terrain the hostiles left an easy trail to follow. There were eighty to ninety animals making tracks across the high prairie of western Kansas, and it looked like a highway had ripped through the virgin country.

"Horse droppings fresher," Eagle Feather said to Winchester. "They get close. Four-hour ride ahead."

Winchester nodded. "We started out five hours behind, so we've cut their lead down an hour. We still might catch them before dark."

By two o'clock they had cut another hour off the lead of the Indians. Winchester called a halt and rested the horses for fifteen minutes at a small creek to let them drink. The men chewed jerky and some hardtack from their rations, then they were riding again.

Captain Cavanaugh moved up beside Lieutenant Winchester at the head of the column. "Lieutenant, you might want to send one of the Indian scouts ahead three or four miles following the tracks to see if he can find any signs of a dust trail. A herd that big is going to lift a ribbon of dust into the sky, and there isn't much wind today."

"Good idea. If they're still three hours ahead, at four miles an hour, that's twelve miles."

"With that many steers and horses, they'll be lucky to make two or three miles an hour," Cavanaugh said. "We're probably a lot closer than we think."

Winchester sent out a scout and they lifted the march back to a lope and followed the trail their scouts pointed out.

By four o'clock that afternoon the troops and the horses were tired, but they were only an hour behind the hostiles. The scouts reported dust ahead, and on a slight rise they saw the herd moving across the grasslands.

Captain Cavanaugh drew up beside Lieutenant Winchester again on his horse. "What's your strategy when we catch them, Winchester?"

"Depends on the situation, Captain. If they leave the livestock and make a run for it, we chase them and leave the stock be. If they try something else, I'll make a tactical decision at that time."

Cavanaugh nodded and returned to his spot beside Lieutenant O'Hara.

Half of the company had been equipped with Spencer carbines, the .52-caliber repeating rifles. The rest of the men had Sharps single-shot .50-caliber carbines. Eventually Captain Cavanaugh wanted every man in the Quick Ride unit to have a Spencer. They could put out a greater volume of fire, and with each man using the same weapon, one supply of ammunition would work for the entire company.

Suddenly, they heard a rifle shot ahead, and galloped for a quarter of a mile, then eased up as an Indian scout met them.

"Cheyenne send back trail scout. Fire at us. The Cheyenne and livestock all stopped ahead one mile."

"Good. They've decided to stand and fight," Winchester said. "Do they have a good defensive position?"

The scout frowned.

"Never mind, we'll be there in a few minutes." They rode at a lope again, and as they came up to the hostiles, they saw the Indians had massed the steers and horses into a barricade in front of them in a small gully that a stream had cut through the rich soil. It had left a wash four feet deep with steep sides that were now almost dry. The Indians could not be seen. Captain Cavanaugh lifted his field glasses and focused on the spot. "The warriors are mixed in with the cattle and horses," he reported. "Looks like they're going to stand and fight and use the cattle and stolen horses as a shield."

The column kept moving forward until they were 300 yards away from the herd. Lieutenant Winchester faced the knot of men, horses, and cattle. His eyes seemed to be staring blankly.

"Lieutenant Winchester, what's our strategy?" Captain Cavanaugh asked when he rode up beside the troop commander.

He looked at Cavanaugh with a puzzled expression. "Company front, dismount and attack cautiously?"

"No, Lieutenant. Troop front, then charge shooting into the cattle and horses, trying to stampede the animals. They won't like the gunfire and should spook easily."

"Yes, yes, good idea." Winchester called out the order for a troop front and Lieutenant O'Hara repeated the order, then each sergeant behind him repeated the order and the men swung out in a practiced move to form a line of troopers and officers fifty-three men wide. The horses were almost shoulder to shoulder and walking forward.

"Trumpeter, sound the charge," Winchester barked. With the second note of the trumpeter's call, the men knew the order and the horses moved out from a walk to a gallop, firing at will into the herd. Discharge of weapons on a charge, while not a usual tactic, would remove the shield around the hostiles by stampeding the livestock to either side.

By the time the troopers were within a hundred yards of the herd, fifteen bawling, wild-eyed steers and a few cows had bolted from one side of the circle, and the hostiles quickly mounted their ponies, ready to fight.

As the cavalry charge came closer, more of the cattle raced off to the side. At the last minute, before the troopers would have plunged into the milling, bawling confusion at the center of the herd, the mounted army men broke around the target, slowed to drop down into the four-foot-deep gully, and then raced up the other side and drove another dozen cattle out of the herd with them.

The riders in blue continued fifty yards beyond the hostiles, then on a trumpet command turned and raced back toward the confused mass of horses, a few cattle and the twelve to fifteen hostiles in the center. This time the trumpeter blew the attack. The men rode in to engage the enemy wherever he was found.

Captain Cavanaugh quickly reloaded with a fresh tube of rounds for his Spencer repeating rifle. He spurred back toward the knot of milling animals and Indians. As he rode, he lifted the carbine and caught sight of a warrior suddenly uncovered by three nervous riderless horses.

Cavanaugh fired from instinct, a snap shot, and saw the savage slam off his mount. He was trampled immediately under dozens of sharp hooves. The blue shirts cut through the mass of horses and steers, pistols out now in the close quarters.

An Indian rose up from behind the trooper's horse and thrust a fourteen-foot-long lance through the man's chest. The private pawed at it a moment, then died and fell off his mount.

Two Indians charged out of the fray and kicked their war ponies up the dry streambed. Four cavalrymen spurred after them, pistols cracking. One of the redskins jolted off his mount and the detail raced around a small turn in the draw after the last hostile.

It was every man for himself. Cattle bawled and charged in every direction. An enormous steer slammed into the side of a cavalry mount. One of the horns gored the corporal riding the horse, the other ripped into the mount's ribs, penetrated her lung, and sent the animal plunging to the ground.

Lieutenant O'Hara jolted into the very center of the melee, held out his pistol, and blew one savage out of his saddle with a .44 round through his forehead. He whirled, sensing something behind him, and barely avoided an arrow launched by another Indian standing beside his war pony. Snapping off a second shot, he saw the redman's throat blossom with a spurting crimson flow as the bullet severed the right carotid artery, sending a geyser of of blood into the air.

A piercing war cry cut through the Kansas afternoon, and the remaining warriors rushed to the upstream side of the creekbed and raced away.

Winchester spurred his horse that way and led a charge with ten troopers after the fleeing hostiles.

As the firing quieted down, Lieutenant O'Hara called on the troops to check the Indians and be sure they were dead so there would be no surprises. They heard two pistol shots and then all was quiet.

"Casualty report," Lieutenant O'Hara called, and the ranking sergeant began checking the men.

Captain Cavanaugh trotted down the gully the way the Indians had fled. He saw Lieutenant Winchester leading his men back. When Winchester passed the captain, he looked up.

"They had too much of a start on us and our horses are about played out." He rode past without stopping.

By sundown, the troopers had rounded up the cattle they could find nearby and herded them back into the dry wash, where they could bed them down for the night. They found only fifteen of the forty horses the rancher said had been stolen. They were put in a small rope corral near the cattle.

"What's the casualty report?" Lieutenant Winchester asked O'Hara as they stood beside their horses.

"We have two dead, sir, and six wounded. The wounded can ride."

"Enemy dead?"

"We've found eight so far, sir. We may find others in the morning. We rounded up fifteen horses and about twenty head of cattle."

"Very well, Lieutenant. We'll camp here tonight. Fires are authorized. See that the wounded are patched up the best we can."

Captain Cavanaugh listened with approval, then went over to a small fire where Corporal Jake Foland wrapped a bandage around a man's arm. Foland had been apprenticed to Major Lassiter while he was at the fort. He and five other men were assigned to learn all they could about doctoring, taking out arrowheads, splinting bones, and wrapping up gunshot wounds.

They were not doctors, but Captain Cavanaugh thought that each company should have one medical corpsman along on every patrol. At times like this, the medical apprentice could do the bandaging; usually it was left up to the wounded man himself or a buddy who could help him. Each of the medics, as they were called for short, had a small medical pack on his mount that contained bandages, scissors, a knife for cutting out bullets, and some rawhide thongs for tying makeshift splints in place, plus whatever else the medic could get from the doctor for his own kit.

Captain Cavanaugh nodded. This was the first time he had seen his medic plan in action, but he was pleased to see it working so well. It should make things a lot easier for the wounded and save lives.

"How's it going, Foland?"

"Good, sir. I've got three more men to go. I do the worst-hit ones first to stop the bleeding. Would it be possible to double the size of my medic kit? There are a lot of items we have lots of back at the medical ward that I could really use about now."

"I don't see why not, Foland. Talk with Dr. Lassiter about the supplies, then come see me and I'll authorize a new medic bag of some kind."

"Thank you, sir. Could you hold this pad on this gunshot wound until I can find some more bandages?"

"Glad to, Foland. I like the way you do things." The captain applied pressure to the thick pad.

"Thank you, sir. I figured saving a lot of blood for Willy here was more important than standing on ceremony."

On Quick Ride patrols and other patrols where hostile action was expected, officers could not take along their orderlies. That meant they had to fix their own food and tend to their own horses. Captain Cavanaugh had instituted the order and found it worked well.

Now he opened his rations from his saddlebag and scowled at the supply: hardtack and salt pork. The salt pork had to be cooked to be safe to eat. Captain Cavanaugh built a small fire and called to Lieutenant O'Hara to come cook with him. First they scraped off the thick layer of green mold, parboiled their salt pork, then fried it in their skillets.

The hardtack was comparatively soft this time, and could be broken by hand, softened up in the mouth, and at last chewed. Captain Cavanaugh had brought along a personal sack of roasted and ground coffee which he boiled for himself and O'Hara. It made rich, strong coffee — if you didn't get a mouthful of the bitter, crunchy grounds at the bottom of the big tin cup. The cup held almost a quart and was handy for most of the cooking chores each soldier had to do in the field.

The two officers talked as they cooked and then ate.

"Was there any way that we could have attacked the savages and not lost any men?" Lieutenant O'Hara asked.

Captain Cavanaugh sipped at the almost boiling coffee, then, gently blew on it to let it cool. "We could have laid off and sent rifle fire into them until their shield was down or they were spooked. But by then it would have been dark and all of the hostiles would have escaped. No, I think the attack was handled in an acceptable manner."

"How would you have done it if you were in command?" Lieutenant O'Hara asked.

Captain Cavanaugh laughed. "Hindsight, Lieutenant, is the simplest game of all. How would you have led the attack?"

"I had it worked out as we rode in. I'd have sent six men in blocking positions up and down the draw, then I'd have sent seven rounds per man into the mass of men and animals. If that didn't stampede the steers, *then* I would have charged them."

"Good, O'Hara, I like that plan. But you still would have lost two men in the charge or in the exchange at your blocking positions. Two men dead on a fight like this is cheap. It could have been six. It could have been you or me. In a battle like this, the luck of the draw plays a big part. Never think that you're bulletproof. Out here, nobody is. Every man can die."

"Amen to that."

Cavanaugh looked out over the scattered troop fires. "How many perimeter guards do we have out?"

"Six. I placed them on three-hour watches, three shifts. That way, we all get some sleep."

"Good work, Lieutenant." The captain put his cup down and stood. "I think I'll check on the men before I turn in. Good night, O'Hara."

"Good night, sir."

Captain Cavanaugh walked through the men as they sat in small groups talking about the battle or singing trail songs. He stopped when he found First Lieutenant Winchester finishing up a supper of a half loaf of hard baked bread and a tin of cheese.

"My private stock," Winchester said quickly.

"And a good one, at that," the captain said, crouching down next to the fire. "Winchester, it's come to my attention that you haven't been giving your second-in-command the respect due him as an officer in the United States Army." Winchester started to protest but Cavanaugh held up his hand. "I won't have any dissention on this post, especially not in Able Troop. The man's a fine soldier and a fellow graduate of the Point. If I hear of any more belittling of Lieutenant O'Hara, you'll no longer be in command of Able Troop. Is this all perfectly clear, Lieutenant?"

The tall officer straightened, a look of shock drifting over his eyes, and he shook his head slightly. "I have to maintain discipline in the troop."

"True, but you find a better way of doing it with your fellow officer. There is no room for argument or compromise here, Lieutenant. Do you understand?"

"Yes, sir." Lieutenant Winchester slumped as Captain Cavanaugh stood and turned away. His brown eyes were dull and he shook his head slightly. He threw the rest of the tin of cheese as far as he could and swore silently. He'd brook no interference in his command, especially from a man he should be outranking by now in his career. *Captain* Cavanaugh still had some lessons to learn about this man's army, and he'd be just the man to teach him.

Chapter Five

Toby Gates sat in the Owlhoot Saloon in the small town of Wallace, population sixty-five but that was only at the Fourth of July county-wide dance. For most of the year, the count was more like twenty, give or take a few drifters and local Indians. The business consisted of the saloon and one small general store that also served as post office, undertaking parlor, and blacksmith shop.

There were three houses in the settlement, if you counted Willy Hedbetter, who lived about two blocks south of town on his small farm that ran down to the Smoky Hill River.

In the saloon, the beer was warm but the talk was free, so now Gates and Willy Hedbetter lifted their glasses in a toast and then set them down on the small table. Two men played a hand of penny ante poker at the only other table in the place. This was a crowd for the Owlhoot.

Willy was a large man, built like a bull moose without the headgear. Broad shoulders strained through a homespun shirt, and his hands dwarfed his mug of beer. He was just over six-feet-two-inches and weighed around 240 pounds. His face was ragged, unshaven for four days, and showing a bruise on one cheek where his woman, Amanda, had clipped him when he'd sassed her. Nobody sassed Amanda.

Willy was twenty-four years old. He was a farmer, and in the last two years had made a living for his wife and two kids and saved nearly twenty-five dollars . . . in cash. Not many in the county could claim that.

Gates had been talking about the Cheyenne raid on the Burroughs ranch eight miles northeast of town.

"You got kin out that way, don't you, Willy?" Toby asked.

"Damn right. My brother, Kenny, and his wife and kid. Trying to raise some cattle out that way. Hell, the big-timers got him beat all hollow. But he tries. 'Course I get a half a beef from him now and again."

Toby Gates screwed up his face and shook his head. "Christ in a bucket, don't know what I'd do if some of them damn heathens got to my family," he said. "I'd go berserk, for sure. If'n some damn Cheyenne come storming in and killed my kin, I'd take off after the sons of bitches with my Sharps Big Fifty, that's what I'd do."

"That so."

"Hell, yes. I'd get my Big Fifty. That sucker can shoot a mile almost on line. It's one of them .50-caliber-by-100 grains of powder models. Heavy as hell but a real head buster. Blow a buffalo down at half a mile. Yeah, think what it'd do to a goddamn Cheyenne, sitting in front of his fucking teepee up there in the hills somewhere. Guess I'd just about go crazy if them Cheyenne got my family the way they did the Burroughs." Gates paused. "What would you do, Willy, if'n something happened to your brother?" he asked as he lifted his beer.

"Ain't gonna. Kenny says he's got lookouts and places to hide and the whole bit."

"Good, good, right idea, living out here so damn close to the danger zone. But say the damn Sioux or Cheyenne slipped up at night or such. What in hell you do then if old Ken shows up, his head split open by a Cheyenne tomahawk?"

Willy squinted his eyes and wrinkled his forehead. Then he rubbed his head and massaged his whole face and ears. At last he looked up. "Why, I guess I'd do just what you'd do, Toby. I'd come borrow your Big Fifty and go do me some Cheyenne hunting. You know, I used to trap up in them hills and places around the Republican and Arikaree. Know that country like the inside of my woman's thighs."

"Hey, Louie!" Gates yelled at the barkeep. "How about a couple more beers over here."

Toby drank with Willy for another hour. Four more times he pounded in the idea that the white man had to stand up to these damn heathens. An eye for an eye, by damn. When Willy surged up to his feet and walked out the door with only a slight weave, Gates grinned. Yeah, he had planted the seed. Now all it had to do was grow.

That same night, Toby Gates packed half of his souvenir Indian short bows and arrows and part of a headdress into a big gunnysack and slung it over his horse. He had picked up the arrows and bows over the past two years in his meetings with the Sioux and Cheyenne to trade for buffalo robes.

He rode out about midnight and got within two miles of Willy Hedbetter's brother's place. It was four miles north of the burned out Burroughs' small spread. Gates eased down from his horse in a brush line formed along a creek heading east. He slept three hours and woke up just after daybreak. Checking his gear and his six-gun, he hurried toward the Hedbetter ranch so he would be in time for breakfast. Only he didn't plan to stay for coffee.

Riding straight through front the yard, Gates tied up his horse at a small hitching rail in front of the house. The screen door slammed and Kenny came out carrying a shotgun. He squinted, "Who in hell's there?" Kenny called.

"Name's Toby Gates. I do some trading with the Indians from time to time. I was talking with your brother Willy yesterday and I thought I'd say howdy on my way up to the tribes."

Kenny lowered the shotgun. "Well, hell. Any friend of Willy's can surely share my table. Come on in and have some breakfast."

Gates walked up to the man and shook his hand, and when Kenny turned to go back in the the house, Toby drew his six-gun and shot him through the back of the head. Kenny flopped onto the dirt by the steps, dead. The killer jumped to the side of the house near the door.

"Was that a shot, Kenny? What's going on out there?" The voice grew louder as the woman came to the door. She pushed open the screen door and looked out. Gates shot her in the heart as she turned toward him.

He didn't figure she'd be so pretty. Damn, he could have used her once or twice first. That was his only thought. No pangs of conscience, no regrets. He jumped inside, found the baby, and shot it in the chest where it lay in a little rocking cradle.

Quickly he ran to his horse and brought back three arrows. He jammed one into each body where his .44 had made a hole. The arrows were hard going in, but finally he had all three driven in far enough to conceal the bullet wound and pin the killings on the Cheyenne.

Then he looked down at the woman. Indians raped the white women, everyone knew that. So he ripped and cut the woman's clothes off, all of them. She had fallen on her back, so he spread her legs to make it look like the Indians had used her.

He scattered around two arrows, and two more broken ones, a discarded bow, which he broke, and then he snagged the piece of feathered headdress on the end of the hitching rail.

Gates worked faster now, riding to the small barn and setting it on fire, and then firing the shed. He'd leave the house. He opened the corral and drove the six horses out. After double-checking that everything looked like an Indian raid, he mounted and headed out.

He rode back toward town five miles, then swung to the east for five miles more so he could come into town from the other direction.

It was the next day before the "Cheyenne attack" on the Hedbetter ranch was discovered. Willy had been due to go out there to help his brother round up some wild horses they had spotted. He found the bodies about noon and raced back to Fort Wallace with the news. Major Owensby and Captain Cavanaugh led Baker Troop out to the Hedbetter place to investigate right away.

At the site they found the bodies where the civilian said they would be. The troops stayed back until Eagle Feather had made a careful inspection of the whole ranch yard and the house.

Major Owensby and Captain Cavanaugh rode up and down outside the house as they waited for the Crow scout to come out. He motioned to them from the door. "Inside, please."

In the tiny cabin he showed them the baby in the crib with the arrow sticking out of it. Then he lifted the child's already stiff form and turned it over. There was a blood-caked hole on the child's back.

"Shot with pistol," the Crow scout said. He put the baby down on the bed and removed some of the blankets and padding from the crib. Underneath the crib, embedded in the hardwood floor, he found a lead slug. He lifted it out and gave it to the major. "Forty-four, forty-five caliber."

Outside, he pulled the arrows out of the man and woman, shaking his head. "Small arrowhead. Bird point. Not for man. Man arrowhead much wide." They turned the woman over and found where a bullet had gone all the way through her body as well.

"Shot, pistol," Eagle Feather said.

He looked around the yard, then at the remains of the two buildings. Stuck in a chopping block at the side of the house were two axes and two small saws.

"Cheyenne raid take axes, saws."

He pointed to half a dozen horses that had grazed their way back toward the corral, looking for some oats or hay.

"Indians raid for horses. Why not take?"

Then the scout found the two unbroken arrows and showed them to the officers. "This arrow, Cheyenne," he said. "This arrow, Sioux. Never Cheyenne and Sioux raid ranch together. Never."

Major Owensby nodded. "So, Eagle Feather, you're telling us that this murder was done by a white man who tried to make it look like it was a Cheyenne raid?"

"Yes. White eye kill all, burn buildings." Eagle Feather went to his horse and mounted and rode around the ranch buildings. Captain Cavanaugh called to one of the Lieutenants about digging three graves. They had brought shovels for that purpose. He put six men on the task near the side of the house.

By the time the graves where half dug, Eagle Feather came back. He shook his head. "Find no tracks of Indian pony raiders. No Indian raiders. Track of one shod horse heading toward town. Maybe day, day and half old. No Indians here."

When they had buried the three bodies and erected simple wooden crosses for the graves, they headed back for the fort.

"That's one we won't have to worry about," Major Owensby said. "Cavanaugh, I want you to ride over to Sharon Springs and report this to the sheriff. You're an on-the-spot witness. Tell him what the scout said, too. Then it's out of our hands."

"Tomorrow?" Captain Cavanaugh asked.

"Hell, yes. Tomorrow."

As soon as Willy Hedbetter got back to town, he headed for the small boarding house where he knew Toby Gates lived. His pounding on the door brought a quick response.

"Willy," Toby Gates said. "Good to see you. Got time for a beer down at the saloon?"

"No time now. My brother Ken is dead. Damn Cheyenne! Cheyenne arrows all over the place. I know their markings. I want your Big Fifty."

"My Big Fifty? Let the Army handle it, Willy."

"No. Got to be family. Eye for an eye. Bring me your Big Fifty. You really got one?"

"Sure, but that's dangerous. You're not going to . . . Oh, no! You remember what we was talking about the other day about going after the Cheyenne ourselves. Drunk talk, Willy."

"Get the Big Fifty for me, and a hundred rounds."

"You're serious, aren't you, Willy?"

"Damn serious. Get the Big Fifty. I'll stop by at my farm for a sack of grub, and I'm heading for the hills. Hell, I know where half those bands have their summer camps and their hunting camps. I can kill as many as I want and they'll never see me. I reckon I owe them at least six — no, nine, just to make sure they remember. Yeah, nine."

Ten minutes later, Gates watched from behind the curtain as Willy Hedbetter stepped into his saddle and cradled the Sharps Big Fifty across his arms as he rode for his little farmhouse south of town.

"Goddamn, it worked!" Gates exclaimed in delight. Now all he had to do was sit back and wait. The Cheyenne hated nothing more than an enemy they couldn't see. Within a week they would be raiding every white eye they could find to try to rid themselves of this "bad magic," this long-gunner who they never could catch.

Willy Hedbetter was fifteen miles north by the time the Army had finished its evaluation of the killings. He did not punish his horse, but he worked the big black as hard as he knew she could stand. It would take him a day and a half to get into the country where the Cheyenne liked to camp. Then he would be more careful. Tomorrow at dusk he would make his first kill, and he wouldn't be too particular about who it was — as long as it was a Cheyenne!

The next afternoon, he worked his way up a creek he called Wandering Stream that emptied into the Arikaree. He had trapped the area years ago. He knew where the heavy brush was and how he could get close to the small Cheyenne band that often stopped there late in the year before the big buffalo hunt.

He rode his horse into the brush, picketed her, and lifted off the Big Fifty and the cloth sack holding the sixty rounds he had brought. He patted his mount but left the saddle on for a possible quick exit.

Then Willy Hedbetter walked swiftly and surely toward where he figured the Cheyenne band would be camped. His heart was hard, as the Cheyenne said. All he could see were his kin, stiff and pale in death with open, staring eyes.

When he parted the last brush on the slope above Wandering Stream, he found a familiar sight. Fifteen tepees lined the little stream. At the far end of the string of brownish-gray buffalo hide covers on the tepees, he could see where the band's ponies were kept.

Fortunes must be down for this band, he thought. He guessed they had no more than forty horses. That would be less than three mounts per warrior. He had seen some Cheyenne bands where the leader had well over a hundred horses all his own.

He studied the closest tepee. An old woman sat outside working on a hide. Two children ran to the stream, splashed and screeched at each other.

A warrior came out of the tepee and went to another. He called, and a second warrior came out and the two men stood talking. Good enough for the first time, he decided. He had already inserted the big round, and now he lined up the sights, judged the distance and the downhill shoot, and adjusted. He zeroed in on the man nearest the tepee.

Hedbetter's eyes watered and he stopped to wipe them. He had only five minutes. Dusk was falling quickly now. Again he sighted in, aimed at the first warrior's chest, and squeezed the trigger. The cracking blast of the high-powered cartridge surprised him. The stock jolted against his cheek. For a moment he couldn't see through the haze of blue smoke from the muzzle.

Quickly he levered out that round and pushed in a new one. When he looked back at the tepee, the man he'd aimed at was flat on his back and not moving. The second man stared at his dead friend, then began to run toward his own tepee.

Willy tracked the Cheyenne Warrior, led him by a hair, and fired. The second warrior stumbled, threw his hands into the air, and slammed backward between the two tepees.

Since the breeze blew toward Willy, the blue gun-powder smoke pushed back into the brush. The Cheyenne would have no idea where the rounds had originated. He lay there watching. The old woman in front of the tepee lay on the ground not moving. The two boys in the stream had ceased their play and sat in the cold water, shivering.

Then a wail came as a woman darted into the scene and fell on the body of the first dead warrior. That brought out another woman, and slowly the band filled the area. Two warriors ran out holding rifles.

Willy eased back from the thick brush opening and ejected the shell casing. He picked it up, as well as the first one, and smoothed out the place where he had lain and his entry to it so there would be no signs for the Indians to read.

He went back to his horse by a different route. As soon as it was dark, he moved cautiously forward, working higher on the Arikaree to a valley where he had found good trapping and where the Cheyenne had driven him out.

Willy Hedbetter looked up at the stars as he rode through the woods and down to the edge of the valley of the Arikaree River. "Those two are for you, Ken, my lost brother. And there'll be more, I swear it."

Chapter Six

Silver Bear, leader of his own band of Cheyenne, had his fall camp at one of his favorite spots high on the north fork of the Republican River in Colorado Territory. They had been coming here every year for the past decade to rest and prepare for their major buffalo hunt.

The fall hunt would provide the buffalo jerky to fill their parfleches so the women could pound the jerky into pemmican. The buffalo provided almost all of the necessities of life for his band, from buffalo robes to sinew for bowstrings. They used every scrap of the animal, even the bones for utensils and tools.

It was a satisfying time for Silver Bear. He had brought his band through another summer of minimal confrontation with the white-eye Horse Soldiers. He had kept the truce with the Sioux bands intact, and there had been four successful raids on white eyes who were trying to push into the Cheyenne hunting grounds.

Soon it would be time to send out scouts to find the thinning buffalo herds and to plan the hunt.

Silver Bear was especially tall for an Indian, standing six-feet four-inches. While the Indians did not use the word "chief," he was a respected leader not only of his own band, but of all of those Cheyenne in the Arikaree-Republican River area. Sometimes he dreamed of a large coming together, when all the tribes, of the area would unite and their warriors would move out and fight the white eye wherever they found him, sweeping the Cheyenne and Sioux hunting grounds free of the hated white eyes for good.

One small band could not stand up to the Horse Soldiers when they swept down from the hills. But a combined force of the Sioux, Cheyenne, and Arapaho would be a big enough force to do the job. They could field 800 mounted warriors. With a force like that they could sweep the white eyes from the entire region.

The Cheyenne leader shifted his weight now where he was seated on a buffalo robe in front of his tepee on the north fork of the Republican. His shield, lance, and bow and arrows stood just at the entrance to his dwelling, where they would be easy to grab if the camp was attacked.

He watched his number-two and number-three wives working on hides. A chance buffalo kill last week had provided fresh meat for the band, and six new hides to scrape, dry, and cure in the sun. Silver Bear heard something and looked toward the end of the camp. A rider worked his way through the tepees and the people. He shouted at some, waved, and then rode for the largest of the tepees, the one with the head of a silver-tip grizzly bear painted on it. The rider, a Cheyenne from another band, stopped at last where Silver Bear sat, and dismounted.

The warrior stood in front of the leader and waited to be welcomed. Silver Bear remembered his name — Running Feet. He was from the band of Long Bow down on the Arikaree.

"Running Feet, welcome. Sit. You've had a long journey." He looked at his number-three wife. "Small Doe, bring food and sweet water for Running Feet."

Number-three wife promptly brought hot stew, along with a clay pot filled with pure, cold spring water. The warrior ate the stew hungrily, savoring the small wild onions in it. When the food was gone, he turned the bowl upside-down, indicating he could eat no more. Then he looked up at Silver Bear and got to the purpose of his visit.

"There is great pain and worry in the Arikaree camps, great leader Silver Bear. Four of our camps have been attacked by a devil firing a long gun. He is like a spirit we never see. We search but can find no trace of him or of any horse he may use.

"He has killed nine of our people. Five warriors are now with their ancient ancestors, as well as three women and a child. The long gun sounds like the devil gun that those who slaughter the buffalo use. He kills just at dusk, then is gone in the night, only to strike again another day at another camp.

"This dusk spirit also has struck at two Sioux camps, and they are furious and preparing to wage war on all white eyes."

Silver Bear watched the messenger. Running Feet was a courageous warrior with many victories, but now he was afraid. Even telling the story made him tremble.

"Warrior Running Feet, there is no spirit that can shoot the white-eye long gun. This spirit is nothing but an angry white eye, or perhaps two of them. They strike at dusk so they can fade away into their friend the darkness and escape when you try to follow and punish them. We must raid in retaliation."

He closed his eyes and thought through the situation, considering the time of year and the months yet ahead when they could do their hunt. "I'll go back to your band with you, and on the way we will speak with as many Sioux, Arapaho, and Cheyenne bands as we can find. It's time we have a coming together of the three peoples in this area to form a powerful force to drive the white eye and his Horse Soldiers from our hunting grounds forever."

That noon, the council of Silver Bear's band met and talked long and loud. Silver Bear presented the plan to call for a coming together of the tribes and bands. Then the warriors spoke. Every warrior was free to speak his opinion.

When all was said, Silver Bear lit the ceremonial pipe and drew hard on it, then passed it around the circle of twelve on the council. All twelve warriors who agreed with the plan would smoke the pipe. Those who were opposed would not smoke. Every warrior on the council took the pipe and smoked.

On the three day journey, Silver Bear and Running Feet spoke with eight different leaders of all three tribes. They arrived at Long Bow's band on the Arikaree and found the band preparing for a raid. They planned to sweep eastward to a pair of farms that had been settled recently and strike back with a vengeance for the two warriors and the child killed in their camp by the long-gun white-eye coward.

During the preparations for the raid, the council met and listened to Silver Bear and quickly approved of his plan for a gathering of the tribes. It would be ten days from that day, and the central gathering place would be the Arikaree River, a half day's ride upstream from where it joined with the Republican.

Silver Bear walked the camp, talking with old friends. He had relatives here who had chosen to follow Long Bow years ago. In the Cheyenne society, any Cheyenne was free to come or go from any band. If a man decided he no longer believed in a leader, he could pick up with his belongings and move to a new band and live there without question or penalty.

He commiserated with the widows of the slain warriors. Both of the dead warriors had had two wives, and now there were four women and three children with no one to hunt for them. One returned to her father's tepee, one went to her sister's husband's tepee and became his third wife. The other two were still waiting, wondering what would happen to them. The women had the customary healing wounds on their arms and breasts where they had slashed themselves in their frantic, terrible mourning. Proper respect must be shown and grief must be loud and painful.

Suddenly, two riders came thundering through the campsite. Both ponies were ridden by boys no more than ten or eleven. Both were working hard at guiding the ponies through the tepees and buffalo drying racks. One of the horses caught the edge of a drying rack and dumped it onto the ground.

The woman who tended it did not even look after the pony and the two boys as they rushed on past. She bent and set the drying rack back up, then brushed off the fallen strips of buffalo meat that were almost dried into jerky and arranged them again on the series of sharp pegs driven into a soft pine pole across the top.

It was the way of the people. Children were almost never scolded and never struck. They went their own way. Sometimes they were given jobs to do. Often the girls were asked to scrape skins. If they did the work, they were praised. Soon they realized there were certain things they had to do to be full members of the band. It made for a carefree and happy childhood.

Silver Bear remembered the raid coming tomorrow. He had brought along his sacred bonnet that he always wore into battle. He was convinced that it gave him total invulnerability to the arrows of other tribes and to the bullets from a long rifle or pistol.

Before doing battle, the Cheyenne leader performed a complicated series of cleansing rituals. He went to the tepee that had been loaned to him for his overnight stay and began the strengthening of his spirit so his magic would be powerful against the white eye.

First he took off his breechclout and stood naked in the tepee. He closed his eyes and turned around slowly ten times. Then he prostrated himself and hit his head three times on the hard floor, offering his earthbound spirit to the Great Spirit.

With that done, he put on his breechclout and took his bow and arrow and walked into the timbered slopes behind the camp. There he sent up prayers and made an offering of a sacred bead from his medicine bundle to the four points of the compass, then prayers to Mother Earth, Father Sun, and his Cousin Moon. Then he sat perfectly still for two hours, legs and arms crossed, to let the spirits speak to him.

As he sat there, two young boys ran past him hunting a badger. They would capture a live badger for the war ceremony later that night.

When Silver Bear returned to the tepee after dark, he was brought food. He pushed it away. One of his taboos was that he could not eat for twenty-four hours before a raid or a battle. He heard a call and went out to join in the ritual of the badger.

The badger the two young boys had caught was held high by Long Bow. He pierced the badger's heart with a knife and killed it. At once he sliced open the belly and ripped out the entrails, then lay the carcass on its back on a bed of sage. The badger would lie there all night and the creature's blood would pool in the cavity created in its midsection.

Just before they left for the raid, the warriors would unbraid their hair and walk by the badger. They would stare down into the pool of blood, looking for their reflections. If a warrior saw himself with white hair and wrinkled with age, he knew he would be safe on this raid because he would live to be an old man. If the warrior saw a man with a bleeding head because he had no scalp, he knew it was a bad omen and he would at once withdraw from the warpath and not go on the raid or into battle that day.

Silver Bear stared at the badger for a moment, wished its spirit well, then went back to his lodge to complete his rituals before he slept. He prostrated himself and prayed to the Great Spirit for an hour.

Afterward, he took out his sacred war bonnet and studied it. He carried it everywhere he went because it brought him strong magic.

His bonnet was really an elaborate headdress almost three feet long. It was made of two pieces of finely chewed doeskin, soft as silk and sewn together. The inside piece had been dyed blue and the outside a rich red. On the sides of the red were worked trading beads making four bands of white, each an inch wide. Between them were twin tepees six inches high.

Four sets of the twin tepees worked down the left side of the headdress. Through the middle, a six-inch wide strip of red fox fur was carefully sewn together so it extended from the top of the bonnet all the way down to the bottom.

The far side of the red-dyed doeskin also held bars made of small white beads, and between them four sets of two lances with bright steel points. Down the middle of the back of the fox fur, twenty-three eagle feathers were pushed into the fox skin and glued in place so they stuck straight out.

Across the top of the war bonnet and covering Silver Bear's forehead was a complicated pattern of colored beads sewn to heavy buffalo hide. Dangling down the sides covering his ears were magic charms, one on each side made from stuffed kingfishers and festooned with beads and feathers. The swift and agile kingfisher bird brought Silver Bear speed, so he could dodge arrows and lances.

Silver Bear cleaned the headdress carefully and hung it on one of the side poles. Then he performed the last of his rituals. He went outside and made one last appeal to his Cousin Moon to protect him in the battle to come. His magic complete, he could sleep deeply.

In the morning he arose early, did not eat anything but only drank water. One by one, the warriors going on the raid rode past the medicine man's tepee. He met each one and waved a long branch over each warrior's head to mark them so the spirits high above could see the warriors and grant each one the strongest magic so he would be brave and victorious.

Silver Bear rode out with the rest of the fifteen warriors. It would take a whole day's hard riding and part of the night before they came to the place where the white eye had built up two of his wooden structures — the white man's tepee. This would be the first of many victories in their war to drive the white man away.

Chapter Seven

Enemy raids were an important part of the Cheyenne way of life. The men had practiced being warriors since they were three years old and their fathers had small bows and arrows for them. To ride into battle or on a raid against a worthy enemy was the sole purpose of a Cheyenne warrior's life.

In days past, a war party might ride for three weeks to get to an enemy. On these trips they took along a few women to cook for them, and they might cover six or seven hundred miles. But now the white man had pushed the Cheyenne higher into the mountains, far from the flowing plains. Their scouts had reported this raid would cover only about "a day and a half ride" to get to the white-eye lodges. They each left with a roll of pemmican around their waist and a few sticks of buffalo jerky to chew on.

Being an honored guest on the raid, Silver Bear rode up front beside Long Bow. They talked as they rode, remembering their youth when they were in the same camp and played at being warriors.

"The old ways are slowly fading away," Long Bow said. "My father never raided the white eyes. He said they were too easy, like killing a wounded buffalo. He enjoyed a good fight but with a man who was as skilled as he was."

Silver Bear nodded. He remembered that one day Long Bow's father had found a Sioux warrior who was more skilled than he was and that he died learning the lesson.

"We make this raid, then we prepare for the Coming Together on the Arikaree," Long Bow said. "How many warriors do you think we can gather?"

"Seven hundred to nine hundred, if we can get word to all of the Arapaho. The Sioux are easy to find, and we will contact each of the eleven bands of Cheyenne in this area."

They rode faster then, racing across the downslope of the last timbered ridge into the sweep of the plains toward the far horizon. Both men talked of the times when their people had been free to hunt and settle in this part of country. It was not long ago that the white man had come to destroy their way of life.

They rested their horses after a four-hour ride. The warriors lay in the shade of small trees along a stream and let their mounts drink and rest. The ponies were smaller than those the Horse Soldiers used, but they were range bred and hardy and could survive on twigs and brown grass, where a cavalry mount would starve.

Soon the small band rode on, replacing their lead scout every few miles. They watched for any formations of white-eye troopers. Long Bow wanted no confrontations with the Horse Soldiers before they had completed their raid.

Just before dark the raiding party hit a small stream and followed it eastward. It was nearly midnight when their lead scout came back and reported, "The first white-eye camp is ten long arrow shots ahead. The second settlement is three times that distance to the right."

They settled down in the trees along the river to sleep and wait for dawn.

At first light, the Cheyenne were up and had put on their war paint. The paint was to frighten their enemies, and to signal to the spirits that they were ready to fight but not to die. It helped to keep them safe in the battle ahead.

Silver Bear put on his sacred war bonnet, and whispers flew around the camp that the great Silver Bear would be invulnerable to all the white man's bullets. His magic would ensure their victory.

The leader heard the talk and he stood in front of the warriors. "I wish you well," he said. The warriors quieted to listen to this great leader.

"I wish you all strong magic. May you gain many horses and captives before the day is over."

Long Bow mounted his war pony, and the others did, too. He lead the party forward with a simple hand signal.

A short time later they saw the white settler's cabin. It was a square box with smoke coming from the top. A man walked out of a small building behind the house. He slipped overall straps over his shoulders and looked up just as the first Cheyenne warrior broke from the brush and fired his rifle.

The shot missed, and the man sprinted toward the back door of the small house. He got within six feet of it when a charging Cheyenne sent an arrow from his bow, which sliced between the man's ribs, instantly killing rancher Neamiah Van Dercoover.

There had been no cry of alarm from the house. Quickly four Cheyenne burst into the corral behind the barn and claimed the six horses there, driving them out and herding them into a group.

Three warriors leaped from their horses and stormed into the house, war axes in one hand, war clubs wrapped with softdoe skin in the other.

One of the Indians came out quickly dragging a screaming woman with long blonde hair. He knocked her down and dropped an arrow beside her, marking her as his property. The woman sat up, groggy from the blow, and cringed when she saw the rest of the painted Indians riding and whooping around the yard.

A moment later she spotted her husband lying near the side of the house. She screeched as she raced to his side and knelt down beside him. At once she saw the arrow through his chest, and tears poured from her eyes as she screamed at the murderers.

Another Cheyenne warrior came out of the house, carrying a stack of dresses, hats, and men's pants. He put them down, placed his own marked arrow on the stack, and rushed back into the house.

He soon returned holding a long gun over his head. He yelled in delight, even though he had no ammunition for it and did not know how to use it. A long gun was prime trading material, worth three horses.

A brave had set the barn on fire, and soon it surged up in one huge mass of flames as the dry hay stacked inside for winter feed went up in smoke. Two cows thundered out of the burning barn and the Cheyenne chased after them for sport.

The third warrior ran out of the house, holding a child in his arms. It was a girl not more than three years old, with long blond hair like her mother. The warrior yelled and grabbed the child by the hair, whirling her around in a circle and finally catapulting her through the air.

The woman shrieked in fury and ran toward her baby. Before she got there, the warrior who captured her, Bent Lance, rushed out and tripped her, then sat on her and whipped his hand across her face twice. She lay there screaming at Bent Lance and at the other warrior who picked up her baby again.

The warrior held the tiny child in the air by her heels and hung her upside down, just out of reach of her mother. He screeched with laughter. Then he bellowed a warning to the other warriors not to touch the child. He held her by her ankles and twirled her around and around, then threw her once more as far as he could.

This time the small girl landed on her head, breaking her neck. Bent Lance roared his anger. It was no sport to throw a dead body. The warrior searched for a tool he wanted, found it, and hurried back to the child's body. He lifted the ax and cut the small head off the body, then kicked the head across the yard and called to the others. The game began, using the child's head as a ball. Someone stopped the game and cut off her hair so the "ball" would roll better, then continued the game.

When Amy Van Dercoover saw the ax fall on her baby, she fainted into the dust of the yard.

After they took what they could from the house and nearby tool shed, two warriors torched the buildings.

An hour after they arrived, the raiders left. Most of the warriors had a bundle of loot they'd retrieved. Among the tools taken were axes, saws, and the greatest treasures of all, files for shaping the metal into arrow points and lance points and sharpening them.

Bent Lance slapped the blond woman, then lifted her onto his horse and sat behind her holding her, in place. The woman twisted and turned and tried once to scratch his eyes. He slapped her again, almost knocking her off the horse. Then he pushed against her nose hard with his thumb. The woman calmed down but cried continuously as they rode to the next small ranch.

This ranch was a cattle spread with three corrals filled with horses, two barns, and a larger house. They paused in the small ravine near the back of the ranch house, and left their booty hidden near the back, along with the woman who they gagged and tied tightly to a cottonwood tree with strips of rawhide.

The warriors surged away from the trees in an undisciplined stampede. They charged the ranch yard screeching war cries, firing the two rifles and three pistols they had.

Two cowhands raced back for the barn and dodged inside. One tried for his horse, but he didn't make it in time and went down with an arrow through his thigh. He rolled behind the corral fence and fired twice with his six-gun. One warrior took a round in the shoulder and spun off his mount. He lay on the ground gritting his teeth, then sprang up and ran to his war pony, which had been taught to stop whenever its master left him.

The warrior leaped on its back and raced at the cowboy with his lance poised in his good hand. Twice the cowboy fired. Twice he hit the horse, but it didn't go down. The warrior kept charging forward, then just before his war pony crashed into the poles of the sturdy corral, the warrior threw his lance. The moment it left his hand he nudged the war pony with his knees and it turned sharply to the left, away from the white-eye gun.

It made no difference. The lance with the four-inch steel point slashed through the cowboy's thin shirt into his belly, slanting upward and tearing up his vital organs. The man grunted, then blood spewed from his mouth and he died before he could get off another shot.

Two warriors had broken windows in the ranch house. One warrior charged in the rear door, only to be blown back into the yard by the blast of a shotgun bearing double-ought buck rounds. He died instantly.

Another warrior crept up beside the door, reached around, and fired his revolver three times into the house. He heard a low moan and darted through the door. A moment later he came out dragging a woman in her forties. She had two bullet wounds in her chest and was dying fast. He dropped her in the dust and raced back into the house, followed by two more warriors.

One white eye from the barn ventured out a few steps when he heard the women scream. He fired at three warriors but missed, and they shot arrows at him and drove him back into the barn.

Silver Bear dismounted and entered the main house. He had not been in many white men's homes and they amazed him. It was strange to him how they could build such a lodge and leave it in one location. There were three large rooms with square images on the wall, and a strange device made of iron that was very hot. The house contained many things to sit on and tables with objects on them. Even beds off the floor. The windows were still wonders to him: sheets of ice he could see through, yet they would not melt from the sun's fierce heat. He picked up a small hand mirror from the room with the beds and walked back outside.

A warrior ran out behind Silver Bear dragging a screaming young woman of approximately sixteen winters in age. She had on no clothes above her waist and was covered with welts and scratches. The warrior did not have his breechcloth on but carried it in his teeth. He rushed into the yard, pushed the girl down and spread her legs, taking her quickly as the other warriors hooted at him.

Long Bow and the rest of the war party were busy dividing up the horses. As the braves chose their prizes, they rode off. Silver Bear mounted his horse and rode past so close he could touch the wood of the barn and threw a torch into the haymow door ten feet off the ground. Flames leaped up in the dry weeds the rancher had put in the barn. Soon the buildings burned fiercely and smoke poured out of the lower doors.

The large front door flew open suddenly and one white eye ran out with his hands over his head. The Indians had no idea what he was trying to tell them.

Every warrior close by who had a bow shot an arrow at the man. Five struck him, three in the chest, and he cried out, then toppled over dead in the dust.

The second man saw what happened. He ran out the back door, shot one warrior who had been checking on the horses, and caught his war pony. The white eye leaped onto the pony, caught the hackamore, and raced off before the warriors in front of the barn realized he was gone. They saw him tearing along toward the east, toward the white-eye towns and the Horse Soldiers.

Silver Bear signaled to Long Bow to end the raid and ride off. He urged his horse to the east. Slowly the warriors picked up their booty and headed for the draw where they had left the rest of their goods.

Both women were tied up and forced on the horses. They begged to put on some clothes. The warriors understood their gestures but refused. They set them astride the unsaddled war pony, the lead reign held by one brave.

The two warriors who had been killed were tied over the backs of their war ponies and attached to a lead line behind another warrior's horse.

When the warriors had secured their goods, they began their trek back to the Arikaree River campgrounds. Six men drove the plundered horses in a herd toward the mountains. Most of the mounts had been broken and were tamed, but four broke away at once and raced into the prairie. The warriors did not chase them. They still had forty-two horses, a great prize for such a brief raid.

They rode the rest of the day, pausing only once more to rest the tough little Indian ponies. The two captive white women were at last given some of the women's clothing that had been stolen so they could cover themselves from the hot sun. One was already sunburned, the other close to it. Their owners bargained for the clothing and got them covered so they wouldn't die on them.

Long Bow was aware that a witness had escaped and that there would be someone on their trail soon. Once they got to the start of the hills and the timber, they broke up into five different groups of three men. Each of the groups took some of the captive horses. If anyone tried to follow them they would find an intermixed mass of trails that crossed, crisscrossed, and turned back on themselves.

The warriors rode through the night until they could smell their camp on the wind. Long Bow sent one messenger into the village to alert them of their arrival, then the warriors camped a short distance from the village. They would reunite in victory the following morning.

With the first hint of daylight came a flurry of action. The warriors put on new war paint, dressed up in the captured clothes, and brushed down their war ponies until they were sleek and clean. Then they ate a meal of pemmican and rode into the band's camp after sunrise.

Every old man, woman, and child was out to greet them. The women wore the best dresses they had, with fancy beads sewn on or rows of elk's teeth that clattered with every move.

The women who had lost husbands wailed and screamed and slashed their breasts and their arms, crying and wailing as they displayed the proper form of mourning. Young girls ran along with the warriors, throwing flowers at them, and women and men alike raised a joyous shout as the men paraded in. Long Bow was at the head of the procession, with Silver Bear in an honorary second position.

They walked their war ponies slowly through the whole camp, showing off the two women captives and parading the forty-two captured horses. Then the procession turned and went back through the camp, this time each warrior turning off at his own tepee, unloading his booty and sending his horse back to the pasture.

As soon as the warriors had rested, the drums began to beat in the council circle. There, a fire was started and the oldest buffalo robe that could be found was laid down in front of where the council of twelve sat. Then all the people in the camp came to hear the tales of battle. When the population had assembled, the drums stopped and a warrior on his horse and wearing his war regalia thundered through a narrow path left in the mass of seated Cheyenne to the front of the gathering where the council sat.

The warrior lifted his lance and sank the steel blade deep into the ground through the old buffalo robe before the council.

Then he stood on the back of his war pony, and with gestures and terrible faces, told a glowing story of his bravery and how he stole ten horses himself, and how he counted coup on one of the ranch hands before he died, and then how he burned down the barn and watched it roar and drive out the white eyes hiding inside.

When he was finished the people cheered and he rode out, and another warrior raced into the circle and planted his lance deep into the buffalo robe and told his own tale of bravery and honor and victory.

This continued until each of the warriors on the raid had told of his brilliance and bravery under fire by the enemy white eye. One warrior told of the game of kick ball with the head of the small white girl, and the women cheered the loudest of all.

After the warriors' telling of the victory, the council moved together to sort out which coups should go to which of the warriors when a coup was contested. They would make the decisions and the warriors would abide by them.

Silver Bear retired from the celebration early and went to his tepee to rest. He was not as young as he had been, and he had started to feel his age. Tomorrow morning he would be back on his pony again, riding with one of Long Bow's most trusted men. Together they would visit four of the other Cheyenne bands in this area, then they would part and each visit another group of camps of both Sioux and Arapaho, until every band in the whole area knew about the Coming Together, now only eight days away.

Chapter Eight

Just after 2 P.M. that same day as the Cheyenne raids, First Lieutenant Scott Winchester led Able Troop up to the small farm and ranch that had been destroyed. The lone survivor had run the Indian pony hard and made it to Fort Wallace, fifteen miles away, in a little over two hours. The Indian pony foundered and died two hundred yards from the fort.

Newt Stockner rushed into the fort and was taken at once to the commander's office, where he excitedly reported the raid to Major Owensby and Captain Cavanaugh. He was given a horse and a quick meal and was ready a half hour later to lead a patrol back to the ranches.

Lieutenant Winchester ordered the bodies buried at both places, then with his scouts pointing the way, led out on a chase after the hostiles. He kept his troop of forty-five men moving at a good clip. By eight o'clock that night he figured they had covered about twenty-five miles heading northwest toward the mountains.

"Damn Cheyenne," Winchester growled as they stopped to rest their mounts. "Damn hostiles don't mind riding a hundred miles to make a raid. Be a miracle if we find this bunch."

Lieutenant O'Hara made no comment. He had been functioning in the troop at a regulation level, but that didn't mean he had to be friendly with the man who had given him so much trouble in his command.

"Will we be moving any further now that it's almost dark, sir?" Lieutenant O'Hara finally asked.

"No. Give the order to make camp along this stream. Put out the usual guards. We'll pursue the bastards another twenty-five miles tomorrow, but I bet we never see a redskin."

"Yes, sir." Lieutenant O'Hara gave the word and the men set up camp at once.

Usually the troops had daylight to establish camp, but now they had to do the best they could in the dark. First came the horses; they set up picket lines for them and fed and watered them. Some of the men rubbed down their mounts and curried them.

Details were sent to gather wood. There was plenty of fuel near the creek where high water had left dead dry wood, good for making a fire.

After the camp was secured and wood brought in, the men started small cooking fires. On the march, each man was responsible for his own food and cooking — there was no company cook.

Each man had been issued five pounds of salt pork and hardtack for the patrol. It was enough food to sustain a soldier in the field for two days. Many of the men said it was enough to kill a trooper after three.

They boiled the salt pork to make it safe to eat, then drained off the fat which they often threw in with the hardtack and boiled them together to make it more palatable. There was no time to cook beans, which could take from six hours to a full night.

Usually each man had an issue of green coffee beans, which he roasted over his fire in his cup or sutler-bought skillet. The beans were put in a small sack and with a pair of rocks pounded into a powder, then boiled for coffee.

One trooper, known to bring along special food when he could afford to buy it from the sutler, had a feast this night. He pulverized hardtack along with bacon and raisins and boiled the mix in his tin cup with condensed milk and a little water. For dessert, he fried moistened hardtack in some salt pork grease, then sprinkled it with brown sugar.

Once their meals were over, the men spent the rest of the night relaxing or playing friendly poker with matchsticks or pebbles, since most of them had little gambling money left over from their $13-a-month wages.

Some of the men wrote letters or kept a diary, and there was always the usual enlisted man's gossip, bitching about the officers and non-coms, and daydreaming about what they were going to do once their hitch was up and they could get out of the damn Army. Private Beauchamp, a trooper from New Orleans, had brought along his mouth organ and played for the men as they hummed along.

The company carried no shelter halves for the small "pup" tents. Each man had his blanket and slept next to his saddle.

As usual, first call from the trumpeter at 4:45 A.M. came much too soon the next day. The troopers climbed from their blankets on the hard, cold ground. Within ten minutes, they came to order and saddled their mounts.

Five minutes later they heard mess call on the trumpet and the men had half an hour to fix their breakfast. Usually this was a cold meal of hardtack and water, or a quick fried salt pork.

By 5:30, they struck camp, stowed all of their personal gear and weapons on their mounts, and prepared to ride. The troops fell into a column of fours in marching orders and waited for the signal to ride forward. Promptly at 6 A.M. Lieutenant Winchester gave the signal to move out along the line of travel that the scouts had found for them.

The ten to fifteen hostiles and the stolen livestock had cut a plain trail across the prairie. There had been no attempt to confuse a tracker so far. The Cheyenne were running as fast as they could back toward their mountain camp and safety, or at least to reach reinforcement from the others in their band.

The march continued through the morning. By the time they had traveled twenty more miles, Lieutenant Winchester called a halt at a small stream to rest the horses. He told the lead scout to call back his two men out in front.

"This as far as we're going?" Lieutenant O'Hara asked the troop commander.

"It is, O'Hara. We've pursued the hostiles for at least forty-five miles. I can see the next six or seven miles up the slant toward the mountains. The savages are not in sight. That makes more than a fifty mile pursuit. Seems like a waste of resources to continue it any further."

"Yes, sir."

"Tell the troops we'll take our noon break here and when we march again, we'll be heading for home."

Back at Fort Wallace, in the commanding officer's office, Captain Cavanaugh and Major Owensby were standing in front of a wall map of the area. The map covered western Kansas and eastern Colorado. It had fairly accurate but unsurveyed boundaries, rivers, streams, trails, towns, settlements, and every ranch and homestead they had managed to track down.

There were red thumbtacks on the black-and-white map marking places where there had been Indian raids involving deaths during the past year. Each red splotch was labeled with the name of the spot, the number killed, the number of horses stolen, and the tribe thought to be responsible.

Cavanaugh had pasted smaller white squares of paper by the red tacks. "These white marks represent attacks within the past six months. Look at the pattern. They're moving closer and closer to our position. That's partly because they've cut down half a dozen outlying ranches, but does this positioning mean anything else?"

Major Owensby pulled at his beard. "Hell, it means we've got a damn rough situation. Looks like the attacks have been increasing. Since I've been here we've had what — five or six?"

"Averages out to one killing raid every two weeks." Cavanaugh set his hands akimbo on his hips and marched around the room. "Don't know if it would work, but what we're doing is reacting to what the savages do. They have the offensive. What we need to do is anticipate their next attack."

"I don't follow you, Cavanaugh."

"I'm not sure that I make sense, either. Just wondering . . . " He stared out the window at a troop working on the drill field. "What would happen if we placed, say, two squads of men or a platoon out in a couple of ranches and waited to see if any savages attacked? We could camp out in some brush or cover along a river or stream to stay out of sight."

"Yeah, it might work. If you were lucky. But hell, they might hit any one of ten or fifteen ranches out that way."

"True. It would be a gamble. But we could pick the most likely. The Cheyenne especially like to go for small ranches where they get a remuda of thirty to fifty horses. That's candy on a string to them horse lovers."

"True. Work up your idea and let's talk about it again. We could call them training patrols. Couldn't hurt one single goddamned thing."

"Yes, sir. I'll check with local general supply for a few suggestions."

Later that day, a trapper rode wearily into the fort and asked to talk to the commander. The Officer of the Day knocked on Captain Cavanaugh's door and showed the grizzled man inside. He said his name was Loot Chalmers and he did some trapping up in the hills to the west.

"Not a lot left in there, but I can do all right during the fall and early winter, then I streak on out of there. Lately things been getting ugly." He spit a stream of tobacco juice into a mostly unused spittoon beside Cavanaugh's desk, hitting it in the center. "I work with the injuns. When I get a good catch in my traps, I skin the critters out and take the meat to the squaws. They'll eat anything. But then, couple weeks ago I got the idea they'd just as soon eat me as the beaver. One of the chiefs warned me to stay away. He told me somebody up in that area around the Republican and the Arikaree been gunning down Indians with a buffalo gun."

"What tribe?"

"Oh, Cheyenne, first one. Big Ear. Usually a right friendly sort, but not anymore. Then I talked to a Sioux by the handle of . . . of . . . Buffalo Piss. He said one of his hunters spotted the shooter and he was a white eye. But this white eye knew the woods better than the brave and got clean away."

Captain Cavanaugh paced his office. "Any idea who this white man might be, Mr. Chalmers?"

"Could be me, but it ain't. I know them woods and hills and streams like my woman's left tit. Have to be some white eye who knows the area."

"Like another trapper?"

"'Pears as how." Loot Chalmers looked around. "Wouldn't have a nip of whiskey now would you, Captain? Man gets mighty thirsty . . . "

Captain Cavanaugh took a fifth of whiskey out of his bottom desk drawer, and two glasses. He poured a little in each and sipped his.

Loot threw down his whiskey in one shot and smacked his lips. "Yeah, ain't had nothing that fine in years. Genuine sippin' whiskey."

"You saying the Indians are up to something?"

"Damn right, Captain. I ain't seem them so riled up in four or five years. Mad as hell, Captain."

"Mad enough to make more raids on us?"

"Yeah, they'll do that. But something else is cooking. Didn't see in their pot, and they wasn't saying, but something big is brewing. Heard that in an Arapaho camp, too, and in a Cheyenne village."

Captain Cavanaugh stared at the worn, dirty, bedraggled old trapper. "Sounds like you're saying the tribes are getting ready to attack with a unified force."

"No, sir, not me, I didn't say that." He took off his black stocking cap and scratched his thinning, graying hair. "I didn't say it, but you sure as old Billy hell did. Don't 'pear to be much else that would fit the puzzle, does it, Captain?"

"Damn!" Cavanaugh stood and strode around the office. "How many do you think are in that area you were working?"

"Around the Arikaree? Damned if I know. Could guess five hundred warriors, maybe. Not sure. Could be twice that many."

"Mr. Chambers, could you get back into that area?"

"Could."

"Would you go back and work as a scout for the U. S. Army at two dollars a day?"

"Two dollars . . . " He looked up. "Hard money? Sixty dollars for a month's work?"

"Right."

Chambers held up his glass and Captain Cavanaugh poured him another shot. He downed it and blinked, shaking his head.

"Be damned. I ain't seen sixty dollars hard money in five years." He frowned, his hooded eyes almost closed under his thick by brows and heavy lids. He rubbed the back of his neck, then shook his head. "Sorry, Captain. I like what hair I got left. Be worth a white man's pelt to go back up there right now. Them Indians are crazy mad."

"I'll make it three dollars a day."

The old trapper grinned, then laughed. "Beats all, Captain, but a man with even ninety dollars in his pocket can't have no fun spending the gold when his head is lopped off and the savages play kick ball with it." He stood. "Just wanted to pass on what I knew. Up to you what you do about it." He looked at the whiskey bottle, and Captain Cavanaugh tossed it to him.

"Thanks, Chambers. The Army will have to do its own scouting work."

As soon as the trapper left, Cavanaugh went in and reported to Major Owensby what the trapper had said.

"You believe him about this sniper, and the possible joining of forces of the three tribes?"

"Yes, sir. Every word. A trapper who won't make himself ninety dollars for a month's work is damn scared. He probably hasn't seen a ten-dollar gold piece for two years. Never seen a trapper who wouldn't go for army gold. Not before now, that is."

"So he's scared but smart. We'll see what we can find out. Any of our Indian scouts who could get friendly with those tribes?"

"Not a chance. The Crow were enemies of all three of those tribes up there."

FLINT
IF HE HAD TO DIE, AT LEAST IT WOULD BE ON HIS TERMS...

Get a taste of the *true* West, beginning with the tale of *FLINT* FREE for 15 Days

Hunted by a relentless hired gun in the lava fields of New Mexico, Flint *"settled down to a duel of wits that might last for weeks...Surprisingly, he found himself filled with zest for the coming trial...So began the strange duel that was to end in the death of one man, perhaps two."*

If gripping frontier adventures capture your imagination, welcome to The Louis L'Amour Collection! It's a handsome, hardcover series of thrilling sagas by the world's foremost Western authority and author.

Each novel in The Collection is a true-to-life portrait of the Old West, depicted with gritty realism and striking detail. Each is enduringly bound in rich, Sierra-brown leatherette, with padded covers and gold-embossed titles. And each may be examined and enjoyed for 15 days. FREE. You are never under any obligation; so mail the card at right today.

Now in handsome Heritage Editions

Each matching 6" x 9" volume in The Collection is bound in rich Sierra-brown leatherette, with padded covers and embossed gold title... creating an enduring family library of distinction.

The major nodded. "You going to try that hide-and-seek idea of yours out at some of the outlying ranches?"

"Yes, sir. It's been a week now since the last raid. We'll head out in another two days and plan to stay for three days."

"Good luck."

The hide-and-seek program was greeted with little enthusiasm by the owners of the two ranches they picked. A man by the name of Harding gave his grudging permission for the troops to camp out in the brush 200 yards from his ranch house.

"I got me a young daughter in there. I spot any one of your men near her, I'll shoot him dead, you understand me, Captain?"

Captain Cavanaugh assured him that the men would not be anywhere near his house or barns unless there was evidence of an attack. Leaving Lieutenant O'Hara there with half of Able Troop, he went on with the other half to the Fanfare ranch, another five miles west in the shadow of Sunflower Mountain, over four thousand feet tall and the highest spot in all of Kansas. The woman of the ranch refused to let him camp anywhere nearby, her husband being on a drive.

"Ma'am, I'm afraid you can't tell me no. We're trying to protect you from the Indians, and we're here and gonna stay here for three days. You best just make the good out of it you can."

Cavanaugh rode with the other half of the troop a quarter of a mile west to a creek with a half acre of brushy woods, and set up camp. Main duty was at night for the men. The captain told them what they were doing and how it would work. The whole troop would be on lookout duty from dark to dawn. They would be stationed around the western side of the woods and report everything they heard, even if it was a coyote call.

The first night went without incident. The men went to sleep in the shade of the trees after a hot meal of boiled beef commandeered from the ranch. Fires this close to the ranch would not be suspect by any hostiles, even if they were close enough now to spot them.

The second night, after another trooper reported hearing a horse, Captain Cavanaugh worked up silently to the edge of the brush and spotted two riders working toward the ranch.

"Advance scouts," Cavanaugh whispered to Sergeant Young. The Indian riders were slowly approaching the ranch house.

Cavanaugh slid out of the shadows and followed them on foot. They came to within fifty yards of the ranch house and sat there until the last light in the windows went out. He watched as the two riders turned and walked their animals quietly back to the west, angling more to the north than the route they had followed coming in, then he returned to his men.

"The advance scouts are on their way back to report to the main force. My guess is that they'll attack early tomorrow morning. The problem is, they'll probably want to use this patch of woods to hide in until they attack."

With daylight, Captain Cavanaugh and Lieutenant Winchester rode around the ranch looking for another hiding spot to the south or east. They found it where the small river curved around the barn and left a brushy strip twenty yards wide and a hundred yards long. They moved the men a few at a time, and well before noon the men were in place. They would sleep the afternoon away, have a good supper, and be wide awake and ready to stand guard until dawn.

Captain Cavanaugh rode up to the ranch house and was met at once by an angry man who was tall and thin and carried a six-gun on his hip.

"What'in hell is this I hear about my ranch being occupied by the damn U.S. Army?" the man bellowed as Cavanaugh stepped down from his horse. "My wife said you even took a side of fresh slaughtered steer the other night."

"We're on a training patrol, Mr. Henderson. But our guard noticed that two Cheyenne or Sioux warriors rode up to within fifty yards of your ranch house last night. Your night guard must have seen them."

"We don't have a night guard. Why would injuns do that and not hurt us?"

"They were advance scouts. Come dawn tomorrow, you'll have fifteen or twenty of their friends paying you a call."

The man frowned. "You just making army talk?"

"Not likely. I expect an attack on your ranch tomorrow morning. You'd do well to have your remuda spread out somewhere so it won't be stolen. I'd appreciate every hand you have to be in the house and barn with a rifle and about twenty rounds.

"We'll be watching all night. There are twenty-four of us. As soon as we can see the savages, we'll move in from our position south of the barn and open fire. It's our hope that we can rout them before they do any damage to your people or property.

"Get your womenfolk into the root cellar or the best fortified part of the house. How many hands do you have?"

Henderson was now obviously shaken. "Hands . . . yes, six, plus two sons and me. Nine. Nine more rifles. We all can shoot some."

"Good. Make things look as normal as you can, but don't walk out in the open come sunup tomorrow."

"Oh, god! I heard about them other ranches. The damn Cheyenne?"

"Or Sioux. Plenty of them north and west."

Henderson sagged. "Damn heathens," he said and hurried back into the house.

Chapter Nine

Most of the men of Able Troop of the 13th Cavalry Regiment slept away the rest of the day. As soon as it was dark, Captain Cavanaugh gave Lieutenant Winchester specific instructions.

"I'm going to go out in front of that little woods up north and west of the ranch house where we stayed before. I want to know for sure if the hostiles come in there during the night. If they do, I'll come right back here. As we discussed, at the first sign of attack we'll lay down a barrage of fire and try to pick off as many of them as possible. Then we'll mount and charge before they can do any damage to the buildings or the people. Any questions?"

"No, sir. Good luck out there." Then Lieutenant Winchester raised his eyebrows. "You're going to *walk*, sir?"

"Yes. You ever hear of slipping away without a sound when you're riding an army mount? Besides, I don't want that gelding of mine to be horse talking with about thirty Indian ponies."

"Yes, sir, I see."

Captain Cavanaugh left the cover of the trees and walked around the ranch buildings. He didn't want some ranch hand's over-eager trigger finger to blast a few rounds at him. He circled the structures and moved toward the woods two hundred yards northwest of the place. When he could see them in the halflight of the quarter moon, he walked straight ahead until he found a semblance of cover. It was a small bush and the beginning of a wash. He could lie down in the wash and leave his head and shoulders even with the rest of the land, but still conceal himself under the bush.

He lay there for hours, then looked up at the Big Dipper. It was working its way slowly around the North Star on its nightly journey. By the position of the stars, he knew it was midnight. Soldiers, cowboys, and wandering minstrels were probably the only ones who used those stars for a watch.

Off in the darkness, he heard a coyote begin his mournful howling. Far off toward the mountains he heard others pick up the call. Then suddenly all the coyote howling stopped.

He listened hard, straining to hear the smallest rustle. For a long time he heard no sound, then soft footfalls came across the silent prairie. He turned toward the sound and it came louder, more distinct but still soft.

Hooves! he thought with satisfaction. Were they coming directly at him? He listened again, then stared toward the sounds. There were still no clouds, but the quarter moon's light was faint.

Then across thirty yards of land he saw moving shadows. Horses — Indian ponies — each with a shadowed rider. They were heading for the woods. Vainly he tried to count them. A dozen, fifteen, twenty? He wasn't sure. They came even with him, then moved on south and east, heading directly for the dark mass of trees along the stream.

He lay there listening and watching. Nothing else moved. He lifted himself up and moved away from the woods, then swung back around the farm buildings. He wondered if he should tell the Hendersons that the Indians had arrived, but decided against it. They would stay more alert this way.

As he came toward his own men, he walked upright without making any noise. No one challenged him. He walked into the brush and saw two men talking, their backs to the ranch.

He touched one on the throat with his six-inch knife.

"Trooper, you're dead!" he hissed. The private's eyes widened in fear. "If I had been a Cheyenne, your throat would be slit and your friend would get a second knife in his belly and die in two or three hours. You're on report, mister! Stay alert!"

Nothing happened until the first faint signs of daylight showed to the east. The troopers had their horses saddled, their weapons loaded and ready. They would fire prone with aimed shots for Indians or their ponies, then mount up and charge on command.

When they saw the first Indians, they were walking their horses slowly toward the buildings. It was just light enough to see.

"Pick a target," Cavanaugh announced, and the command went down the line of twenty-four troopers. "On my command," he said.

The Indians were 30 yards from the buildings. Some of them were masked by the barn.

"Two rounds, fire!" Captain Cavanaugh bellowed. The carbines barked, then the men scrambled into saddles.

"Forward . . . hoooo!" Captain Cavanaugh yelled. Then almost at once, "Charge, fire!"

The wave of twenty-four troopers and officers swept toward the ranch buildings. The Cheyenne had charged into the yard as soon as the rifles were fired. Now Cavanaugh heard firing from the men in the barn and house. The Cheyenne ran around in confusion, more used to surprising an enemy than being surprised.

Captain Cavanaugh lifted his Spencer and fired quickly at a Cheyenne who galloped toward the ranch house with a torch in one hand. The carbine .52-caliber round struck him in the chest and drove him off his mount, the torch blazing harmlessly on the dirt.

The line of cavalrymen swept forward. Some of the Indians saw the blue shirts coming and turned and galloped away. Others were not so quick to see the danger. The troopers parted as they came to the barn, swung around it and the corrals, and charged straight at the Cheyenne still mounted.

Carbines gave way to revolvers as the soldiers fired at the redskins. The six-guns barked, and four of the Indians fell, mortally wounded. Four more mounted warriors slanted around the house and fled north.

Cavanaugh bellowed at four troopers near him. "Follow me!" he barked, and they swung to the side with him and the five of them chased the retreating savages. Riding without holding onto the reins, Captain Cavanaugh brought down one of the Cheyenne with a well-placed shot from his Spencer. A trooper knocked down a horse and the other two Indians split up, heading off at sharp angles to each other.

Signalling to his left, Cavanaugh led his men in hot pursuit of the survivors. One of the Indian ponies hit a soft spot in the plains and stumbled, pitching the warrior over his head and into the grassy plains. The two cavalrymen nearest the downed rider pumped shots at the Cheyenne. One of the .45 rounds struck home and the Indian's face erupted in a spray of blood.

Cavanaugh swung his horse around and galloped back toward the ranch buildings. He was almost there when one Cheyenne came racing toward him from out of the barn. By the time he turned to look ahead he was face to face with five cavalrymen. Three carbines barked and the redskin flew off his pony and never moved again after he slammed into the dust.

Troopers milled around still mounted, looking for more targets as Cavanaugh and his men returned to the yard. Lieutenant Winchester came riding up, a strange look on his face. Cavanaugh ignored him for a moment until he was sure the fight was over. He counted six dead Indians.

"Sergeant York, check the hostiles and make sure they are all dead."

York saluted and walked toward the Indians lying on the ground.

"Well done, Lieutenant," Cavanaugh said to his second-in-command. "How many got away?"

Lieutenant Winchester swallowed hard, then found his voice. "Four, maybe five. They won't be telling any victory stories in the tepees tonight." He looked relieved that the fighting was over.

"Take charge of the men and form them up over by the barn. Get a casualty report. I didn't see any wounded, but there might be some. I'll check on the civilians."

The captain rode to the front of the ranch house. Two men came out on the porch, big smiles on their faces.

"By damn, we gave them sons of bitches a hot welcome," one young man said. Behind him came the owner of the ranch.

"Any of your people hurt, Mr. Henderson?" Cavanaugh asked.

"Just some cuts from flying glass. We lost two windows, but that's about it." He walked over and held out his hand for Cavanaugh to shake.

"I want to thank you. I was a blamed fool for getting angry with you. How'd you know the damned injuns would come here, anyway?"

"Didn't. Just took a chance. We covered another ranch, too."

"Glory! How many we kill?" the young man asked.

"Seven, eight, maybe nine. Should be some Indian ponies around, if you want to round them up. They're smart and tough."

"Might try that," the youth said.

"Damn, now I guess we got to bury these corpses," Henderson said, looking around at the Indians they'd killed.

100

"I reckon," Captain Cavanaugh agreed. "You tell me where and I'll get some men to start digging, if you can spare a shovel or two."

The younger Henderson boys stripped the bows and arrows and feathers off the dead Indians for souvenirs. Men from the barn saddled up, hooked ropes onto the Indians' ankles, and dragged them out to a common grave the troopers were digging a quarter of a mile from the house.

Later, the two officers sat in the ranch house kitchen and drank coffee and talked with the ranch couple. Henderson's wife heated up some cinnamon rolls she'd made the day before.

"How many horses do you have on your ranch, Mr. Henderson?" Cavanaugh asked.

"All together, I'd say about sixty. We do some trail driving to the railroad."

"Sixty horses is a prize the Cheyenne will come after again and again. Best to keep them spread out around your ranch. Then maybe they'll bypass you. Staying alive should be worth it. We can't be here every time you need us. We were lucky this time, we all agree on that," the captain added.

The troops rode out of the ranch about an hour later, heading for the Harding ranch to pick up Lieutenant O'Hara and his twenty-four men, who had seen no action. They all rode back for the base together.

"I missed it!" Lieutenant O'Hara blurted when he found out about the attack.

Cavanaugh laughed. "You'll have plenty of chances to get your hands bloody, O'Hara. They just happened to come our way this time. Luck of the draw."

"Then, I'm asking for a re-deal," Lieutenant O'Hara said and grinned.

Captain Cavanaugh chuckled. The kid was going to be just fine. He was thinking of putting him in charge of a special group that would get out of the fort quickly to answer Indian raids. Quick Ride. He liked the sound of that. Supply them with minimum equipment so they could move fast and hit hard. Plenty of ammunition, no excess baggage. He'd talk to the major about it.

They reached the fort before dark, in time for mess call. Captain Cavanaugh sat down beside Lieutenant O'Hara.

"I've got an idea I want to talk to you about, O'Hara. It's called Quick Ride." He went on to lay out the basic idea, and the young lieutenant had an idea or two that fit into the captain's plans.

Later the talk turned to the fight.

"Have you ever seen Lieutenant Winchester flinch in battle? You've been with him on a couple of fights before, as I recall." Captain Cavanaugh watched the lieutenant closely.

O'Hara looked up quickly. "I'm sorry, sir, I really can't answer that question. If there's any behavior I think is putting the troop in jeopardy, I'll be sure to let you know about it."

Captain Cavanaugh nodded and Tim got up and excused himself. The captain wondered what it was he had seen in Winchester's face today. Was it stark fear, or just a queasy stomach, or was it something deeper? He wasn't sure. The way Tim had looked when he'd asked him about Winchester had told Captain Cavanaugh a lot.

Lieutenant Winchester would bear some watching in the weeks to come. Some damn close watching.

Chapter Ten

Every working morning at the fort, the executive officer, Captain Cavanaugh, had a conference with Major Owensby. This morning they looked at the morning report, noting again that they were just a little over half strength on men and ten percent better than that on officers.

"In Chicago, they told me not to expect any more troops or officers," Major Owensby said. "Still can't get used to it, but this is field operations, so I guess I should. What else have we got?"

Cavanaugh went over to the wall map and studied it. Major Owensby had put a new red tack on the board at the Hendersons' to show where the last Indian raid had been.

"If those Cheyenne came from the south fork of the Republican River, they rode sixty miles to get to that ranch," Cavanaugh remarked. "One old Tonkawa scout we used to have told me he knew of raiding parties that would ride four-hundred miles to make a raid, then turn around and rush right back to the home camp."

Major Owensby lifted his odd plumed hat from the corner of his desk and put it on. Today he wore a private's shell jacket and sergeant's striped sky-blue regulation pants, and a thick plaid shirt. He grinned and sipped at a fresh cup of coffee. His beard was getting longer.

"Cavanaugh, you're setting me up for a pitch about how we need to make longer patrols, right? So go ahead and tell me about it."

"It's time we take the offensive, Major. We're authorized to retaliate after raids, but the orders also say that we need to maintain the safety of the Smoky Hill trail into Denver, and the well-being of the settlers.

"We need some scouting reports, but we can't send one or two men into that territory and expect to see them alive again. What I think we should do is send a large patrol, say two troops, up toward the Republican. It would be a show of force. We wouldn't necessarily look for a fight, but we could let the damned savages know we're ready and waiting for them. We might be able to send out some of our Crow scouts to see what the villages and camps of hostiles up in there are doing. Whether they're settled in for the winter, getting ready for a fall buffalo hunt, or on the move."

Major Owensby lit a long black cigar and puffed it until it glowed red at the tip. He leaned back in his chair. "Trouble with you, Cavanaugh, is you never allow a man any room to argue. You throw up so many good reasons, a man is hard put to find a

105

reason to say no. Hell, yes, let's give it a try. Take whichever troops you want to. You seem partial to Able."

"It's got a lot of good men in it, and I have some special plans for them that I want to talk to you about later. What I want to set up is a Quick Ride team, about thirty troopers, two sergeants, and two officers, who can be in the saddle and off post fifteen minutes after we get an alert of an Indian attack."

"How you gonna work that? Fifteen minutes?"

"We've got some ideas, Lieutenant O'Hara and I. My suggestion is that we take A and F troops on this patrol and leave just after noon mess call today."

"Why the long delay?"

In the outer office, Major Owensby sent runners to the two troop orderly rooms and the machinery swung into gear. The quartermaster would issue ten pounds of salt pork and hardtack for each trooper. There would be no supply wagon. The men would fall out for troop inspection at 1 P.M.

Captain Cavanaugh led the patrol. Lieutenants Winchester and O'Hara were with A troop, and First Lieutenant George Immelman led F troop.

When the two troops rode out they made a long column of fours as they wound across the high prairie to the west. They would generally follow the Smoky Hill River for about twenty-five miles, then slant northwest and cross the north fork of the Smoky Hill, heading for the south fork of the Republican River.

The Arikaree the old trapper had talked about was another thirty miles north of the headwaters of that branch of the Republican. There wouldn't be time to get all the way up there on this patrol. Maybe on the next one.

Everything was normal during that first afternoon's ride. They had five Crow scouts along. Captain Cavanaugh had the head scout, Eagle Feather, ride with him. They talked about the chances of two scouts hunting on a patrol like this across this country, to feed a patrol of thirty men.

The old scout grinned. "Bow and arrow?"

"Sometimes. Well, far away from the hostiles it could be your carbine."

At last they agreed that two Crow hunters could supply the men with enough meat for one good meal a day. Cavanaugh smiled.

"Good, now take another scout and go out and show me what you can do. I want pheasant or grouse or even a jackrabbit for my supper tonight."

The Indian scout laughed, delighted, and rode off toward the second scout in the trio stretched out ahead of the main party.

That night Cavanaugh and the other three officers ate roasted rabbit and fried prairie chicken along with their hardtack. Lieutenant Immelman was married and his wife always sent him out on patrol with sandwiches and a loaf of bread. He brought out the loaf and cut it into four large slabs, and the men had a feast.

The column began riding at daybreak the next day, heading northwest around the back side of Sunflower Mountain toward the north fork of the Smoky Hill River. They rode hard and made good time. They had a noon break on the banks of the Smoky Hill and then headed for the south fork of the Republican.

The sky was Kansas high that afternoon, soft fleecy clouds drifting far up in the blue. The sun was warm even though it was September, and the men rode in good spirits. Eagle Feather had two of his men out hunting, and Captain Cavanaugh had cautioned them that now they must use only bows and arrows, no firearms.

In the late afternoon, the lead scout came racing back and spoke to Eagle Feather, who rode at once to Captain Cavanaugh at the head of the column.

"Sioux ahead. About forty. No women or children. Look like raiding party."

"What direction?"

"Riding straight at us."

Captain Cavanaugh looked around for some cover. There wasn't a creek or brush line or gully within two miles.

"How far away?"

"Half of one mile."

His men were riding up a small rise. Once over the top they would be able to see the Indians — and the Indians would see them.

"Form a company front, both troops on line," Captain Cavanaugh said to his sergeant. "No bugle, pass the word. Do it now."

Shortly, the 110 men spread out across the prairie with the horses shoulder to shoulder as they walked slowly forward. Soon they came to the end of the rise and Captain Cavanaugh halted the patrol and rode ahead to peer in front of them.

He saw the Indian party casually walking their mounts forward across the high plains. He would allow them to get within fifty yards of the rise, then act.

When the hostiles reached his action point, Captain Cavanaugh moved his troops forward to the crest of the rise where the Indians could see them.

For a moment everything seemed frozen, then the Indians charged.

"Fire!" Captain Cavanaugh ordered. He motioned to his trumpeter to be ready. After the Spencers had spat out four rounds each, he called to the bugler, "Sound charge!"

The bugle call echoed across the high prairie and the cavalrymen surged forward, the outer ends of the line bending inward, every man shooting whatever he had that would fire. Men reloaded their Spencers on the gallop. Others put away their long guns and drew their six-guns, waiting for a target.

In the first volley of fire, two of the hostiles went down and two horses were hit, rearing and throwing their riders. The Indians galloped forward and to the side, a few even turning to retreat not liking the two-to-one odds. The masses of the two sides came together in a screaming melee of pistols firing, horses bellowing, and men falling off mounts.

Lieutenant Winchester flinched as the battle started. He had surged forward, but Lieutenant O'Hara had been watching him. Halfway there he had slowed and then turned to the side and rode behind the troops, away from the battle.

As the forces met, a dozen Indians broke through the single line of blue, and now two of the Indians raced after the single officer riding slowly away.

Lieutenant O'Hara saw them and flashed after them, killing one with his Spencer and riding down the second one just as he was drawing his bow to fire at Lieutenant Winchester's back. He knocked the rider off his horse and fired three shots with his revolver, killing the hostile. O'Hara returned to the main fight, killed another Indian, and took an arrow in the shoulder before the fight was over.

Captain Cavanaugh put down one of the Sioux, then suffered an arrow in his mount's rib cage. The animal slowed to a walk, then crumpled. He drew his Spencer and fired twice with his pistol as a Sioux charged toward him on his pony. The first slug grazed the redman's shoulder, the second thundered into his forehead and erupted through the top of his head with a large portion of his skull. Horses screamed, men bellowed. Pistols blasted, and now and then a Spencer or Sharps carbine barked. The wings of the line had folded in, nearly surrounding the smaller force. Now the Indians began their retreat, driving for the hole in the north end of the blue wall.

Lieutenant O'Hara yelled at half a dozen of his men and they surged toward the open space, cutting off four warriors who had run out of arrows and advanced with long lances tipped with steel. One cavalryman laughed at a redskin warrior, but he took too long to fire his pistol and when he pulled the trigger, it misfired. An instant later, the three-inch-wide steel blade, four inches long and backed by a ten-foot-long shaft, daggered into the private's chest, smashed two ribs, and drove all the way through his heart and right lung. The trooper clung to his horse a moment in death, then slid off to the side.

The Sioux who had thrown the lance started to flee, but O'Hara shot him as he surged past, then chased two more Sioux who were galloping away. Their small, fresher Indian ponies were faster than his heavier cavalry mount, and soon Lieutenant O'Hara returned to the main battle scene. Blood ran down his left arm, which hung limply by his side. The arrow still stuck in his upper arm.

Now most of the action was over. One more warrior rode off the side of his horse, giving no target to two amazed cavalrymen as he galloped away to the north. The cavalrymen milled around, most of them on horses, some leading their mounts. Two men huddled over a friend who had been shot with an arrow.

"Where's the troop doctor?" one of the troopers called out.

"Corporal Foland! Front and center, now!" O'Hara shouted. The trooper with the oversized pack and a shoulder bag ran up and saluted. "Get all the wounded in one spot so you can figure out which ones to treat first," O'Hara ordered.

"Yes, sir." Corporal Foland drew his pistol and fired it twice in the air. In the resulting stillness he called out, "Wounded over here, now! Those who can't walk, sing out and I'll come see you." He turned to the officer. "Sir, I better take care of that arrow now."

"Do the men first, Corporal."

"Let me decide that, Lieutenant. You're bleeding too much. Step down here, please."

Lieutenant O'Hara shrugged and stepped off his mount, then almost fell, but the corporal caught him. He sat the officer down and cut open his shirt. The arrow had gone all the way through the fleshy outer part of his arm. The corporal notched the arrow shaft with his knife, then broke it in half. The motion of the arrow shaft brought a yelp from Lieutenant O'Hara. Then, so fast the officer hardly felt it, the corporal pulled the broken shaft through the wound. He wrapped the officer's arm quickly with a long roll of bandage from his bag.

"Should keep you for a couple of days, sir," Foland said and moved to the next man in the line of wounded.

Three more troopers walked up, one limping, two others holding shot-up arms.

Captain Cavanaugh watched the scene for a minute, then looked for Sergeant York. "Sergeant, give me a casualty report."

"Yes, sir," York said and hurried around to find sergeants to report on their squads.

Captain Cavanaugh counted three troopers dead on the field. Lieutenant Immelman rode up. Cavanaugh looked at him.

"Immelman, find your top sergeant and have him check to be sure that all of the hostiles are dead. We don't want any surprises."

Then the captain looked for Lieutenant Winchester. He had not noticed him in the battle. For a moment he wondered if he was one of the dead, until he saw him standing beside his horse at the far edge of the battleground, looking out across the prairie. Cavanaugh walked over and cleared his throat.

"Lieutenant?"

Winchester didn't turn. "Yes, sir."

"Was it bad?"

"Yes, sir . . . it . . . it was bad."

"What happened?"

"So many died. Killed. It hit me hard, sir."

"Happens to all of us now and again. You'll feel better tomorrow. Just stay here until I figure out what we're going to do."

"Yes, Captain."

Cavanaugh walked back to the center of the battlefield. Things were getting organized. Some sergeants called their squads to fall in and report casualties. Some took a quick roundup report. A Crow scout came back and reported through Eagle Feather that he had followed the Sioux for four miles. They were still moving north. They probably would come back for their dead after dark. "Sir," Immelman said, returning, "we found fourteen dead hostiles. There are four dead Indian ponies and three dead army mounts. I've sent out two men to round up some of the Indian ponies. We can use them to transport our own dead back to camp and let their horses be used by troopers. I'll bring the first army mount I can find to replace yours."

"Good, Lieutenant. Stay around a minute."

Sergeant Long came up and saluted. Captain Cavanaugh returned the salute.

"Sir, in both troops we have four dead, three severely wounded. One of those critical, the medic says. There are six walking wounded who can ride. That includes Lieutenant O'Hara with an arm wound."

"Thanks, Sergeant." He dismissed the man and turned to find Eagle Feather. "How far to a camping spot by a stream?"

Eagle Feather scowled a moment, stood in his stirrups and looked to the north, then south. "Two miles south and to the east."

"Send two men to check it out quickly." The Crow turned and waved at one of his men and they rode south together at a gallop.

Captain Cavanaugh pulled a silver-pocket watch out of his sky-blue pants and opened the face. It was 3:32 P.M. He estimated that the actual battle with the Sioux had lasted about four, perhaps five minutes.

"Lieutenant Immelman, assemble the troops in marching formation and let's see what we have left. Oh, and get me that mount."

One of the sergeants hurried up with an army mount for Captain Cavanaugh. The captain wiped blood off the saddle and mounted. In their preparation to move on, the men had to tie the four dead troopers over the captured Indian ponies. The ponies were tied together in one lead line held by a sergeant who took charge on their way back to camp. The troopers whose army mounts had been killed took the mounts of the dead men and joined their place in the troop.

A fifth trooper died as the men stood in formation. His body was loaded on a pony and added to the sergeant's lead line. Captain Cavanaugh rode over to where Corporal Foland sat beside one of the seriously wounded. Foland stood and motioned to the captain a few feet away.

"Sir, Wilson can't ride. If we move him even on a travois, he's going to die. Maybe two hours, maybe three. I'll stay here with him. The other man is Morales. He can stand a travois. Could you have somebody make one at that brush line over there and send it back for an Indian pony to pull?"

"Sergeant Foland, I certainly can. You just earned another stripe. Congratulations. I'll leave four men here for your company and protection. We should get a travois back before dark. If we don't, build a fire out of sage or grass so we can find you."

"Yes, sir. And thank you."

"You earned it, Sergeant. Carry on."

Captain Cavanaugh detailed four men to stay with the new sergeant, leaving the man's horse and two of the Indian ponies that had been captured.

Then he rode up to Lieutenant O'Hara and said, "Lieutenant, you see any reason why we shouldn't move out to last night's camping location?"

Lieutenant O'Hara hesitated. He started to say something, then obviously changed his mind. "No, sir, no reason whatsoever, Captain."

They sat at the front of the column of fours. Captain Cavanaugh looked at the officer, frowned for a minute, then decided to take it up later. He lifted his hand, turned, and called out, "Forward hoooo!"

The other officers and non-coms repeated the command, and the long line of troopers headed for the woods three miles away. They met Eagle Feather and the other scout about a mile from the stream. He waved them forward. The area had been cleared of any hostiles.

At the campsite the troopers stopped in place and Captain Cavanaugh went to the center of the line and shouted out his praises for the men.

"You acted like real cavalry troopers today, men. I'm proud of you. We lost five men, probably six, but we took down fourteen hostiles and sent the rest bleeding back to their lair. We also saw the benefits of having a trained trooper along who can attend to the wounded. Today Jake Foland was promoted to sergeant, and should be so addressed from now on."

The men Foland had bandaged gave a cheer. Their sergeants scowled at them.

Captain Cavanaugh nodded. "We'll all give the man a cheer when he gets back with his final patient. Is there anyone here who has ever built a travois?" He waited, and two of the troopers held up their hands. "You two men, front and center." They rode forward and stopped in front of the captain.

"Commanders, dismiss your troops to prepare camp."

Shouted commands came from the officers, and then sergeants and the troops broke up and set up a picket line for the horses. They began caring for the animals first. A cavalryman without his horse wasn't a soldier. The horses came first on every march.

Captain Cavanaugh looked at the two soldiers. "We have a wounded man out there who needs a travois to get home. I want you men to build one now and tow it out to the battle site as soon as possible."

"Yes, sir, Captain," the older of the two men said. "We'll need some rope and a hatchet if anybody's got one."

"Sergeant Long," Captain Cavanaugh said. "Help these men get the materials they need."

"Yes, sir." The three men rode away.

Five minutes later, the four officers met near the water where Captain Cavanaugh had called them together.

"I've decided that we'll overnight here, then move back to the fort tomorrow. I've learned most of what I wanted to. The Indians are moving. Now the Sioux are raiding far from their camps. Something has stirred them up. It very well may be this lone wolf sniper who is terrorizing the camps up around the Arikaree River. We'll return to the fort, and in the meantime, I want both of these troops to take target practice. Every man thirty rounds every day for the next four days. Your troopers have to learn to hit what they shoot at."

A little later, the two volunteers towed a travois across the prairie toward a small bonfire they could see in the approaching darkness. The travois was made with two long poles that extended just beyond the horse's head. They were harnessed securely around the animal's neck and held in place with multiple strands of rope. Behind the horse, a platform had been built between the poles. Rope had been used to tie a crosspiece between the poles to hold them apart. More rope was used to form a webbing between the poles. On this were four army blankets. The wounded man would lie there and sway on the cushioning rope springs.

At sundown, the travois came into camp and the wounded man called to his buddies.

"By damn, I ain't dead yet, you polecats. Warn't for Doc Foland here I damn well would have been."

The wounded trooper was taken off the travois and put on a bed of soft leaves and small branches. "Doc" Sergeant Foland sat beside him until he drifted off to sleep after eating his evening rations.

A trooper slowly led an army mount into the area. On the mount's back lay the sixth dead soldier from the battle.

The troops ate a solemn meal that evening, and when the bugler played taps, the men took off their hats.

Chapter Eleven

Toby Gates kicked up his feet on the table in his house and lifted his glass of whiskey. "Just like money in the bank, Foster. You hear how somebody been blasting the Indians? Trapper guy came through here yesterday spouting about it."

"Somebody really shooting them up in their own villages?" Byron Foster asked. The sutler stared at his partner and sipped his whiskey.

"Remember we talked about wishing the injuns would get riled so the army would move in and clean them out of our little valley up there? Looks like that just might be happening."

Toby grinned. "Hear tell Willy Hedbetter used to be a trapper up that way 'fore he started sod bustin'. Cheyenne done in some of his kin week or two ago. Maybe he ran off up there and is whaling away."

"Never can tell about Willy," Byron said.

Toby emptied his glass and smacked his lips. "Soon enough now we gonna fetch us all sorts of expensive whiskey and good-looking women and anything else we want, thanks to the U.S. Army."

"Maybe. But I don't put much stock in army planning."

Toby ignored him. "I think it's time we head back up there and see if the damned Cheyenne done moved out of our little valley where our gold mine is."

"You mean right soon?" Byron asked.

"Yeah, right soon, like tomorrow morning. You tell your old woman to mind the store, and we'll high tail it out of here long about daylight. Bring grub for three or four days and another one of them big canvas sacks."

"You ever get that other ore assayed?"

"Hell, no. Where am I supposed to find an assayer around here? Got to go damn near to Denver to find one. We'll assay it just before we sell it and get rich. Now you get on home and load up one of them good horses of yours and meet me here at sunrise."

"Really think we should go with the injuns getting so riled up thataway?"

"Hell, yes, or I wouldn't have said to do it. Now git! I'll see your ugly face in the morning." Toby grinned as he added, "Hell, Byron, we're gonna be rich!"

The partners rode all the first day toward the northwest, and then all the next day, and came into the hills behind their claim about dusk. They had spotted no Indians, and evidently none saw them. They worked their way silently through the timber and down the far slope until they found the rock monolith. No one was camped there. Nothing had been disturbed.

They hid their horses, bedded down in the deepest brush they could find, and by sunup were at the upthrust beside the tall rock slab.

"Damn, she looks better than I remember!" Toby crowed. "Don't see how we can do less than be millionaires!" He looked down the stream. "First off I want to go down to the Arikaree valley and see if I can spot any Cheyenne or any smoke, case they got a camp downstream."

Gates came back an hour later, grinning. "Watched both ways and didn't see any redmen. No smoke came up from the trees along the river, upstream or downstream. Looks like they headed into the plains to find a herd of buffs. Sure hope so."

He looked at the vein of gold where Byron had pushed back the brush. This time they had a cold chisel, a five-pound hammer, and a long steel rod with a raised cross cut into the end. It was called a star drill.

"Way you work this is to put it against the rock and hit it hard with the hammer. Then one man turns the shaft here so the star is halfway around and we hit it again. That way this steel will bite into the hardest rock a little bit at a time, and after enough hits and turns and hits, you start drilling a hole in the rock.

"Seems like a lot of work," Byron said.

"Hell, yes, it's a lot of work. You don't earn a thousand dollars a month mining gold by loafing around."

"A *thousand dollars a month?*" Byron asked in awe.

"Hell, yes. Easy. Once we get these Indians out of here and can settle down with a crew of men and build ourselves a stamping mill and then a processing plant to separate out the gold."

Foster looked up and scowled. "All that? I figured we could just chisel some out and go sell it."

Gates shook his head. "Not quite that simple. But we can cut out some of that pure looking gold vein right now. Give me that hammer."

Toby whaled away with the hammer and chisel and cut out some of the gold vein, then ran into rock.

"Look at that! Damn near pure gold! I never seen anything like it before. Just one ounce of this gold is worth twenty dollars and sixty-seven cents. One pound is worth over three-hundred-and-thirty dollars! Think what it would be if we had half a wagonfull!"

"Lord a'mighty, I can't even cipher up that high," Byron said.

Toby worked on the face of the upthrust, pounding it with the heavy hammer. "Want to try to get more of that surface rock off," he said. "See if the vein goes both up and down right here."

A good-sized chunk of the rock broke off and they saw where the streak of yellow continued down to the ground level. Toby sat back, panting from swinging the hammer.

"Money in a bucket! You ever in your life see anything that pretty? Makes a good-looking woman seem like a hog. Damn, but that is nice!" Toby shook his head, admiring the gold.

"Let's fill up that bag we brought. No sense going home empty-handed." He brushed back his shoulder-length hair, and his watery green eyes glowed.

121

"Damn, I'm a millionaire, and I can't get to it because of the Indians!"

He chipped off some more of the rock and gold ore. "Christ, if old Willy Hedbetter don't do the job, I'll try something else."

Foster looked up, curious. "You know something about Willy heading back into the hills?"

"Told you I'd take care of it. Now dig some more of that paydirt out of there. I'm going to check the valley. Don't want them hair-lifting Cheyenne sneaking up on us."

"Thought Willy came up here 'cause his kin got slaughtered by some Cheyenne," the sutler said, staring hard at Gates. "Oh, good Lord and Savior . . . it couldn't be. It was you, not the Cheyenne, who killed Willy's kin out on his farm place. You did it purposeful so Willy would go crazy for the Cheyenne!"

"Stop talking and get back to digging. I'll go look for the scalping Indians."

Gates trotted down the edge of the creek along a deer trail heading for the Arikaree River. He peered out cautiously through some brush when he got there. For a while he saw nothing, then far downstream he caught a wisp of smoke, then another. There had to be some Indians there, probably camping about two miles down. They couldn't hear the hammer on steel leastwise, Toby decided. He checked the other way upstream and discovered no Indians in that direction either. He trotted back to the upthrust.

Foster had the canvas sack almost full of chunks of gold he had chiseled out and pieces of rock with the gold in them. He looked up at once and lifted the five-pound hammer.

"Toby, you kill Willy's kin out at their farm? I got to know one way or the other right now."

Toby shrugged. "Look, Foster, you're just a partner, not the boss. I don't like taking orders, and I don't owe no explanation. But I know Indians and what gets them in a fighting mood. Nothing riles them up like getting shot at in their own tepee. They think their camps are safe. So we had to get somebody to hit the Cheyenne and Sioux right in their camps."

Foster declined to look at Gates now and busied himself with the ore.

"You listening to what I'm telling you, Byron?"

"Still waiting for a yes or no answer."

"So it had to be Willy. His kin was the trigger to setting him off on a rampage."

Foster seemed to sag. His shoulders dropped and he reached for his six-gun. "Gates, you murdered that man and woman and child in cold blood and made it look like Indians. Right?"

"Hell, you wasn't doing anything. Yeah, right." His own hand hung over his revolver on his belt. "You gonna do something stupid now that we're almost rich?"

Tears squeezed out of Byron's eyes. "Knew them folks. Liked that little woman." His hand shook over his weapon, then gradually eased away from it. "You're a murdering bastard, Toby. I never shoulda got into this mess with you."

"Hard luck, storekeeper, you're in it. Now you want to get rich or not? I didn't ask you to do in none of them, did I? Just shut up your yap and fill that sack. I saw some injun smoke down a couple of miles. Could be some of the bastards around here yet."

Byron tossed the chisel to Toby. "I'll go keep watch. You finish filling the damn sack." Byron stalked away downstream, but shot one last angry stare at Toby first. "I got to do some thinking on this."

"Go ahead," Toby called. "Just remember, you was in on it. Sheriff can hang you for them three just as quick as me. I'll claim you was with me even, and you poked it in the woman before you done her. You start thinking rich, not go soft like some old worn out whore."

Byron charged ahead down the trail. He was so angry he could hardly see. He brushed tears from his eyes and tried to get control of himself. He had been so close to shooting Toby on the spot that it scared him. That would throw everything away.

But murder, three murders! It shook him. He sat down halfway to the valley and held his head in his hands. After a short while, he stood and walked on down to the edge of the Arikaree valley. He saw the smoke downstream. As he watched, three warriors on their war ponies came out of some brush and worked slowly across an open spot as they headed downstream along the river toward him.

"Damn Indians," Byron whispered to himself. He jogged back up the small valley and told Gates what he'd seen.

"Hell, we better load up and get out of here."

"Neither horse can carry a man and that sack of gold up over the ridges the way we went out last time," Byron said. "We got to go through the valley or leave the gold here."

"We take it. We can wait until dark and slip out."

"Maybe work through the brush along the side of the valley," Byron suggested. He wanted to get away from the Indians at almost any cost.

"Let's try it. If it don't work, we wait for dark."

They packed up, loaded the sack of gold on the bigger horse, Foster's Big Mike, and led the animals down the trail and then into the brush upstream on the Arikaree, where they had to go to get to the easy valley and pass that led east.

A half hour later they were in a tangle of brush and vines and berry bushes that simply would not permit them to break through.

"Let's leave the horses here and check on the damn Indians," Toby said. They crawled to the edge of the brush on the edge of the big valley and stared in disbelief.

A cottonwood tree grew at the side of the Arikaree where the stream bent close to this side of the valley. Around the tree were about twenty Cheyenne warriors, engaged in some kind of ceremony.

"A damn rite of manhood. A torture ceremony, where they judge how strong and pain-proof and brave their young men are," Toby said. "They let me sit in on one once where they hung these boys from pegs through the skin on their shoulders. Damn near killed the kids, but they passed without one yelp of pain."

"How long does it last?" Byron asked nervously. "When can we get out of here?"

"That's the trouble. Lasts most of the day. We're stuck here for a while." He paused, squinting hard at the warriors. "Well, damn, they got a prisoner, a white man. You got them field glasses?"

Byron got them from his saddlebags and looked at the prisoner of the Cheyenne.

"Holy shit! Take a look," Byron said, thrusting the binoculars at Toby.

Toby adjusted the binoculars and looked. "It's Willy Hedbetter! They caught him."

"Looks like it. They gonna torture him to death, right?"

Gates didn't have to answer, because it started right then. The warriors stripped Willy naked and pushed him spread-eagle on his back. They tied him down and cut off his eyelids so he had to stare at the sun with no relief. After his body turned deep pink from the sun, they cut him free and put him in the center of a circle of warriors.

Each time he tried to break out they sliced him with their knives. Soon he had slashes over half his body. The cuts were only deep enough so he would bleed, but not bleed to death.

One of the warriors threw a rawhide rope over a branch on the cottonwood tree and lowered it almost to the ground. Beneath this rope the warrior built a small fire.

"Savages!" Toby hissed. "I heard of this, but never seen it. Ain't pretty neither."

"What they gonna do to him?" Byron asked.

"Watch. You'll find out."

Hedbetter's hands were tied firmly to his sides with wet rawhide. Then more wet rawhide was tied around his scrotum and his forehead. At last he was hoisted by the rope that had been tied around his ankles and positioned head-down three feet over the small fire.

Willy's black hair hung straight down from his head. He swung and twisted, trying to get away from the heat of the fire.

"He gonna bleed to death?" Byron asked softly.

"Be a blessing if he could," Toby replied mysteriously.

A minute later Byron understood. One of the warriors loosened the twisted rope and let the trapper slip a foot down toward the fire. Willy screamed as his hair gushed with flames and burned off, leaving a black stubble and a blackened scalp, then fainted.

One of the warriors swung him away from the fire, and another Cheyenne threw water in Willy's face to bring him back to pain-filled consciousness.

"God! They gonna leave him there?"

Toby shook his head and pointed.

Now the victim was lowered another half a foot. Then the warriors added sticks to stoke up the fire. Willy screamed again, his jagged, terrified cry of torment and agony knifing through the woods and valley. Byron couldn't keep the tears from coming. He shook his head as he watched.

"Ain't right, nohow," he said. "Ain't right that Willy got to go through that. We caused him his grief. We should be out there."

Toby laughed. "Go ahead, run out there and try to rescue him and get captured. Then the warriors will have two heads to boil, 'stead of just one."

As the heat from the fire built up, the rawhide around his scrotum tightened, squeezing Will's testicles like a powerful vice. The heat intensified on the now bare and blackened skull of the man, and his screams came softer and softer until at last they stopped.

More water was splashed into Willy's face and he writhed on the end of the rope. The fire blazed higher and Willy gave one last terrible, guttural scream and passed out again.

Water wouldn't help now.

The fire blazed higher. Now they could see blood beginning to drip out of his ears, then from his nose. A gout of blood gushed from his mouth and a slow keening began among the warriors and gradually increased in volume and pitch as the blood flowed faster from his head. The blood inside his skull was boiling.

Just before the keening reached its peak, Willy Hedbetter's skull exploded like a dropped melon. Blood, brains, and skull fragments showered the warriors.

The keening stopped. Someone swung the body like a pendulum. When at last it stopped swinging, the warriors left the spot and went back to the two young men who were passing their test of pain.

Toby looked at Byron. "Don't even move," he whispered. "We just lay here without a sound until it gets dark and pray that the damned savages are heading back to their camp so we can get out of here." Byron Foster knew he had never been more frightened in his life. If he got out of this, he'd forget all about the gold. Hell, Toby could have it. What good was a whole mountain of gold if you got caught and hung upside-down and had your brains boiled out by some friendly Cheyenne?

By late afternoon, the ritual was over and the warriors began moving downstream. The two young men who had performed the ritual of bravery had to be helped onto their horses. A warrior walked alongside each one so he wouldn't fall off his pony. Soon the shores of the Arikaree River were cleared of all signs of the Cheyenne, except for the slowly swinging body of Willy Hedbetter.

"We should give the man a decent Christian burial," Byron said as they lay there, muscles cramping, bodies demanding water.

Toby snorted. "You want to be the one to go out there and cut him down and dig a grave? Don't talk foolish. Out here, it's every man for himself. We can't help Willy any, nohow. We just sit tight till dark, when it's safe enough for us to get out of here with our gold and our hair."

Foster mounted in back of Gates, leaving the ore sack on Big Mike, and they rode into the very edge of the valley and around to the second creek, then upstream where they turned toward the easiest pass through the hills.

It took them a half day longer to get back to Wallace. They lugged the canvas bag into Toby's house and lit a lamp. Byron picked out four of the biggest chunks of pure gold he could find. He guessed they might weight two pounds.

"This is mine," Byron said. "The rest of it is yours. Forget I ever knew you. I'm not going anywhere near that place again. I'm selling you my half share in the mine for a handshake. I won't say anything about Willy Hedbetter, you got my word on that."

"Damned pleased about that," Toby said. He took Byron's hand, gripping it hard, then jerked the man toward him. Toby's left hand held a six-inch-long knife which he plunged up to the hilt into Byron's belly.

The sutler gasped and his eyes went wide.

"Can't take your word for not saying anything about Willy's kin," Toby said. "Hell, I know you understand." He pulled the knife out and drove it into Byron's chest, over his heart, and saw the lights go out in the man's eyes.

Chapter Twelve

The morning after Captain Cavanaugh presented his formal plan for a Quick Ride platoon to Major Owensby, it came back to his desk marked, "Go get them savages!"

Cavanaugh sat a moment savoring the situation. He was pleased whenever one of his ideas filled a need. After all, he had decided while still in West Point that the Army would be his family. His mother had died when he was young, and his father, a judge in Michigan, died while Cavanaugh was in his first year at West Point.

He found Lieutenants Winchester and O'Hara and showed them the plan. He told them what would be required, and both men seemed enthusiastic.

They would create a special platoon out of the forty-eight men of Able Troop. Thirty men and the two officers would make up the fighting unit. First they would ask for volunteers, then select the rest of the men they needed. They wanted no one overweight or too large, since that would slow down the horse the man rode, and the unit would be only as quick as its slowest man.

Lieutenant Winchester posted a notice about the volunteer platoon on a bulletin board at the end of the barracks and said he would talk to the men about it at the afternoon drill call.

When Winchester left, Captain Cavanaugh looked at Lieutenant O'Hara. "The other day on that patrol, you seemed about to tell me something about Lieutenant Winchester. Now that you've had time to think it through, is it something that I should know about?"

O'Hara looked away for a moment, then sighed. He nodded. "Yes, sir. It sure is. At the fight when we ran into that raiding party of Sioux, Able Troop commander turned from the conflict and rode away."

"He ran from the fight?"

"I'm not sure if he ran away exactly. It could have been some rear-end strategy to cut off stragglers after the fight. All I know is that he turned from the battle just before we closed with the enemy and rode away. He did not even try to protect himself."

"How was that, Lieutenant?"

"He rode at right angles to our attack, and when two Sioux broke through our assault line and galloped toward Lieutenant Winchester, he made no move to escape or defend himself. It was lucky I spotted them and got there in time to kill them myself."

"When I talked to him after the battle, he looked strange," Captain Cavanaugh said. "He kept repeating something about so much killing, so much killing."

"Perhaps the pressure of leading these patrols has taken its toll on him."

"Maybe, O'Hara. If I knew that for sure, I'd relieve him of duty and send him to Omaha for an evaluation. But I can't be sure." The captain hesitated. "There is a way, but it would ruin his career."

"I've been thinking about that, sir. I could accuse him of cowardice under fire and relieve him of duty for the safety of the men."

"Then I'd have to act. Are you ready to do that, Lieutenant O'Hara?"

"No, sir. I've had six months duty here. Lieutenant Winchester's been in the Army for six years. If a court martial didn't agree with me, it would be the end of my career, as well as his."

"Let's let it ride. We'll try to present a realistic training exercise and see how he reacts."

Training was the key word for the next four days. They experimented to see how light they could travel. The ceremonial saber was left off and extra clothes were reduced to one pair of socks. Ammunition was adjusted so each man carried 120 carbine rounds and fifty rounds for the new Colt Peacemaker revolvers that were coming in.

Captain Cavanaugh talked with the veterinary sergeant in charge of the stables, and they determined that the easiest pace for the average army mount was the lope, somewhere between a canter and a gallop. With the lope, the horse had an easy, natural motion that could be sustained for long periods of time without exhausting the animal. By using

132

judicious periods of walking for ten minutes at a time, the lope and walk could produce six miles of travel an hour.

They went on two practice rides, just Captain Cavanaugh and the veterinary sergeant. The captain chose two horses at random from the stable and had them saddled, but with no field gear. They covered a measured mile six times with the lope-and-walk regimen, and checked the time. They had done the six miles in an hour and four minutes.

Captain Cavanaugh met with the quartermaster, Sergeant James Quinn. The captain explained what he was trying to do.

"What is the average number of pounds of equipment carried by a mount in the field with all regulation gear?"

"Sir, just slightly more than 100 pounds for a five day march."

"I want it cut to fifty pounds at most."

The quartermaster shook his head slowly. "Not possible, sir. The McClellan saddle weighs fifteen pounds itself. Add the halter and bridle and that's another five pounds. Then the carbine, sling, and swivel are another ten pounds. That's thirty pounds already. Three pounds of oats a day for the horse. Five day patrol, that's fifteen more pounds and we're up to forty-five."

"Sergeant, you have a list of standard equipment and the weights?"

"Yes, sir."

"Let's look at it and see what we can cut out." A minute later, Captain Cavanaugh looked at the list:

Halter, 2 lbs.

Surcingle, 1 lb.
Saber and slings, 5 lbs.
Waist belt, plate, 1 lb.
Pistol, holster, 3 lbs.
Carbine, sling, 10 lbs.
Carbine cartridge box, 1 lb.
24 rounds Carbine ammo, 2 lbs.
Pistol cartridge pouch, 1/2 lb.
12-round pistol, 1 lb.
Watering bridle, 1 lb.
Bridle, 3 lbs.
Saddle, 15 lbs.
Saddlebags (empty), 2 lbs.
Rations, 11 lbs.
Replacement clothes, 4 lbs.
40 rounds ammunition, 4 lbs.
Forage sack, 1/2 lb.
Oats, 15 lbs.
Lariat and pin, 3 lbs.
Overcoat, 4 lbs.
Brush and shoe pouch, 1 lb.
Curry comb and brush, 2 lbs.
Horseshoes and nails, 2 lbs.
2 blankets, 7 lbs.
Saddle cover, 1 lb.

Captain Cavanaugh looked at the list in amazement. "Over a hundred pounds of equipment and feed, plus the man?"

"Yes, sir. But there are things we can cut down on."

"We won't be taking overcoats, and if it's a three day patrol, we'll have nine pounds of oats," Captain

Cavanaugh said. "We'll live off the land, so we'll need the minimum in the forage pack."

"You probably won't want saber and slings, but you'll be carrying more ammunition."

Captain Cavanaugh looked at the list again.

"We'll also cut the watering bridle, saddlebags, brush and shoe pouch, curry comb, horseshoes and nails, one blanket, saddle cover, carbine cartridge box. How much do we save?"

"About thirty-six pounds, sir. But you say you want a hundred twenty rounds of carbine ammunition per man. That's an additional eight pounds. Then if you go with fifty rounds of pistol solid cartridges, that's another, two pounds extra . . . Overall you're saving twenty-six pounds."

"I'll settle for that."

Sergeant Quinn wrote down the list of items to be eliminated and the number of extra cartridges and gave it to Captain Cavanaugh, who took it to Sergeant Long.

The men for the platoon were selected, and the following morning they went on their first training ride. Captain Cavanaugh heard some rumbles when the men were not issued any rations. They were told it was just a training ride.

Three scouts went along with the thirty men who had volunteered, or been selected for the new duty. Both the troops' officers were along. Captain Cavanaugh angled the troops out of the fort at 6:05 A.M. and picked the gait up to a lope. He rode up and down the column of fours, shouting to the men that this was the gait they wanted to maintain.

"Feels damn strange, Captain, with no saddlebags and no blanket up front," one corporal shouted.

"Get used to it. We're saving twenty-six pounds on equipment. Your horse will thank you come sundown."

They rode for a timed thirty minutes at the lope, then walked for five minutes and brought the pace up to a lope again. None of the mounts faltered, none fell behind. At the end of the first hour, Captain Cavanaugh consulted with Lieutenants O'Hara and Winchester, and they determined that they had covered almost six miles.

Just after they left the fort, two of the scouts had faded away to the left and moved out ahead of the main party. They were to meet on a tributary to the Smoky Hill River called Little Joe, that came into the larger stream in the midst of a large grove of cottonwoods that had got the name of the Hanging Woods.

The meeting place was nearly thirty miles upriver from the fort. If the troop could maintain the six-mile-an-hour pace, they would come to the rendezvous at approximately eleven o'clock.

The sun was warm that September morning, and the troops were sweating before nine o'clock. Captain Cavanaugh called a break under some trees to rest the horses and let them drink.

"Thirty minute rest for the animals," Lieutenant O'Hara called out to the thirty men. He knew every one of them by name, first and last, and how long most had been in the Army. Only two of the men had served less than a year. A few of them were raw boned and thin veterans of the calvary, and were delighted with this new twist to the Horse Soldier's routine.

"Might even get to like it, exceptin' if we got to fight after about three days of this," one veteran said and lifted his eyebrows.

Three more hours of hard riding, loping, and then walking, and the Quick Ride platoon arrived at the Hanging Woods. They saw smoke from the woods, and Captain Cavanaugh moved the men into a Troop Front as Eagle Feather rode into the woods to investigate.

He was back in no time giving the forward sign, and Captain Cavanaugh rode in with the special platoon.

The platoon's two Crow scouts were working on a trench about eight feet long. They had built a fire in it and were filling it with wood to make a bed of coals down the length of the depression.

Lieutenant Winchester rode up to the scouts and demanded to know what they were doing. They pointed to Eagle Feather, who was leaning on his carbine, watching the men.

Lieutenant Winchester dismounted, led his horse to drink, and picketed him, then went to Captain Cavanaugh.

"What in hell are those Indians doing?" Winchester asked him.

"Call the troops around and I'll tell them all at once," Captain Cavanaugh said. A few minutes later the sergeants brought the men to the fire trench. By now, there was wood burning the length of the eight-foot trench, which was about a foot deep.

"You might wonder what's happening here," Captain Cavanaugh said to the men. "On the other hand, you might wonder why you didn't draw any rations. Almost time for our noon chow call."

137

He waved to Eagle Feather, who motioned to the two scouts. They ran into the woods and brought back twenty-five freshly killed pheasants. The heads were chopped off but the birds were otherwise intact.

"On these Quick Ride missions we might not want to carry an extra twenty pounds of food per man. Oats are heavy enough. We can do without rations as long as we have our Crow friends along. Today for noon mess you each get your fill of fresh meat. How does that sound?"

The men cheered.

"Now watch how the birds are prepared and cooked. You might need to do the same thing some time."

The scouts slit the belly open on the pheasants and stripped out the entrails, piling the birds to one side with the feathers still on. When all were ready, they built up the fire a little more, then let it burn down to an eight-foot-long shimmering bed of coals. The pheasants were placed directly on the coals, feathers and all.

As soon as the birds were put on the fire, one of the scouts covered them with dirt taken from the trench. Soon all of the birds were covered up on the coals.

"Men, take care of your mounts, rest up, and in about an hour assemble back here and try your hand at Eagle Feather's field cooking."

Lieutenant Winchester lay in the grass watching the stream near the other two officers. "How much weight did we save by leaving the saddlebags off?" Winchester asked.

"Twenty pounds," Lieutenant O'Hara replied.

"I've never ridden this far without saddlebags," Winchester commented with a touch of discontent. "Just doesn't feel natural."

"That's why we're doing this test run," Captain Cavanaugh explained. "I want to see how the troops react to the changes, see if there's any more weight we can shed, and see if we need anything that we've left behind."

An hour later, the troops began to gather with their mess kit cups and skillets. The issue mess kit was almost universally discarded by the troopers for a six-inch fry pan and a quart-sized tin cup bought from the sutler's store.

One of the Crows began digging off the dirt covering the first bird. When the feathers showed, he stuck a knife into one bird and held it up. Eagle Feather used his knife to slit the bird's skin and peel it off, taking the charred feathers with it and leaving a juicy, well-cooked bird. Each cooked pheasant was given to two men, who were to skin, clean, and divide it.

Captain Cavanaugh licked off a drumstick and smiled. "All this needs is a little salt, but I guess a body can't have everything."

"Catch," Lieutenant O'Hara said.

Cavanaugh looked up and caught a tiny salt shaker with paper over the screw on top. He took off the top, removed the paper and salted his bird, then passed the salt shaker to Lieutenant Winchester.

"The lad does have some good qualities," Winchester said, and the officers all laughed.

They made the return trip to Fort Wallace covering the thirty miles in five hours and twenty minutes — a sixty-mile march in eleven elapsed hours.

Captain Cavanaugh told the major about the trek over supper in the fort commander's quarters. His orderly had fixed a ham dinner.

"So you think this Quick Ride system will work, Cavanaugh?" the major said after hearing out his junior officer.

"Yes, sir. We need a little coordination now for saddling horses and placement of the thirty mounts, but that's just routine housekeeping."

"Good, but it'll have to wait a while. I received some new orders while you were gone today. Dispatch rider came in on the stage. Division says we're to 'redouble' our efforts to stop any threat we hear about any Indian tribes forming military alliances.

"That damn lone wolf sniper seems to have stirred up the tribes at just the wrong time. From what the trapper said, the Arikaree valley is the trouble spot where they might gather. I'm authorizing a troop-sized patrol to head up there in two days. No rush, so go fully equipped with a full troop. Plan on about six days. Make a sweep of the valley and push all the Indians out of there."

"I'll be glad to lead a sweep like that, Major."

"Wasn't thinking of you leading it, just picking the troop."

"We don't have an officer with enough experience to lead it, sir. I'd like to go, and take Able Troop."

"Been working them pretty hard lately, haven't you, Captain?"

"The other troops have been drawing field time, too. They do the regular patrols. The men will rest tomorrow and we'll leave at six-oh-five the next day."

"You want to take a supply wagon and a doctor?"

"No, sir, just our medic, Sergeant Foland. He's better than a surgeon for this kind of a ride."

"Suit yourself, Cavanaugh. I need a full report to send to Division headquarters in two weeks. That give you enough time?"

"We'll sweep that valley clean and be back in five days."

"Not a chance. Draw rations for six."

Later that night, Captain Cavanaugh told both the officers of Able Troop about the assignment. Winchester simply nodded and walked away. Lieutenant O'Hara frowned and looked up at the captain. "You think he should go? Sounds like we've got nine chances out of ten of hitting some skirmishes with the hostiles up there."

"You think a battle with the hostiles might set him off again?"

"I don't know, Captain, I just don't know."

Captain Cavanaugh went back to the Regimental headquarters and opened the personnel history files of the officers. He found Lieutenant Winchester's folder and read through it, noting his various duty posts. He slowly realized that this was the first post where Winchester had been exposed to any Indian fighting — any combat of any type. Before, he had been at Division Headquarters, then in the quartermaster slot at an Illinois post, and in administration in a fort in South Carolina. He was a garrison soldier, not a seasoned frontier officer.

In the upcoming campaign, Cavanaugh would have to keep his eye on him.

Chapter Thirteen

The patrol to sweep the Arikaree River valley pushed off at 6:05 A.M. from Fort Wallace, Kansas, that Tuesday morning. The full complement of Able Troop went along, including Sergeant Foland as their enlisted medical sergeant, three Indian scouts, and both regular officers. Captain Cavanaugh was in command.

The troops were fully equipped, with twelve pounds of salt pork and hardtack and eighteen pounds of oats for the horses.

They rode steadily, crossing the north fork of the Smoky Hill River the first day, and then Beaver Creek in the afternoon. They pushed beyond that ten miles, then called a halt for the night's camp late in the afternoon.

The troops went through the rituals of the trail, picketing the horses, brushing them down, feeding and watering them. Then they built fires and worked on their own single cooked meal of the day.

Eagle Feather came in with three jackrabbits, and Captain Cavanaugh called in the troop's sergeants and gave them the rabbits to divide and cook as they pleased.

Lieutenant O'Hara made one last inspection of the four guards and gave a thumbs-up sign to Captain Cavanaugh, who saw the signal and nodded.

The second day went without incident. Late in the day, they passed through a narrow ravine into the broad valley of the Arikaree. It was just dusk and they had pushed to get into the valley before full darkness. They set up a quick camp in some trees at the edge of the river and put out guards.

"Too dark to check for smoke from any hostiles," Lieutenant O'Hara said. "We could send our scouts out to take a long-range look."

Captain Cavanaugh shook his head. "We'll be able to tell a lot more about whatever they find out if we wait until morning. Let's give the men a good night's sleep."

The camp settled down with no fires allowed. The troops ate soaked hardtack, along with any personal foodstuffs they brought along. The night passed quietly.

At daybreak, a guard's warning cry echoed through the small camp. Indians had invaded the area.

Every trooper came up with his weapon. At the small rope corral where the troop's fifty horses were gathered, the guards saw warriors stealing some of the mounts. They fired, driving off the savages, but not before several horses were stolen.

At once the men saddled the remaining mounts and prepared to move. Captain Cavanaugh saw his tactical situation immediately. He was in a 300 yard wide valley with high grass. A riverbed more than 150 yards wide ran through the center, but it was sandy and nearly dry. Through the middle of it ran a shallow stream that parted to expose an island about 20 yards wide and 60 yards long. It was covered with scrubby alder, some willow and wild plum, and a single tall cottonwood. He looked at the cliffs around them and saw Indians everywhere, hundreds of them. They hadn't closed off the entry to the ravine yet, but they would have plenty of time to do so. It was a trap.

Just then twenty mounted Indian warriors charged from downstream at the disorganized group of soldiers. The way was open to retreat to the ravine.

The troopers who rushed to that side drove off the attackers, killing one and wounding a pony. But they needed some cover, Captain Cavanaugh reasoned, some terrain to fight from. The island. It would work as well as anything in sight that wasn't already occupied by the enemy.

"Regroup on the island out in that shallow riverbed!" Captain Cavanaugh ordered. The sergeants picked up the command and began splashing through the hock-deep water to the small island.

The forty-eight men reached it, ten of them without horses. The thirty-eight horses were brought into a circle on the outer rim of the island and tied to bushes. They formed a living breastwork.

"They knew we were here," Lieutenant O'Hara said. "Must have seen us yesterday and got their war paint on last night. How many of them, do you suppose?"

"Three hundred, four hundred, and we probably haven't seen them all," Captain Cavanaugh replied. "Tell the men to dig in, if they can. Use their mess cups, bayonets, anything. Get some protection."

The orders rang out and the men needed little urging.

A half-dozen redmen charged from one side, but six men with rifles managed to drive them off, wounding one.

"I'd say we upset their plans," Captain Cavanaugh said. "From what I saw, they intended to drive away our horses, then charge us in force and run us down one by one."

"What's the battle plan, Captain?" Lieutenant Winchester asked.

"We repulse them however we can. O'Hara, put five men with Spencers up there on the point of the island. That's how they'll try a mass attack, if they make one."

O'Hara ducked into the troops and picked out his best shots, sending them to the point, where they crawled through the lush, tall grass until they were almost at the water line. They formed a "V" facing front so all could fire at once.

Rifle fire came now from the cliffs along both sides of the little valley. Horse after horse whinnied loudly as they were hit by gunfire and fell dead. One private took a rifle round through the head.

Captain Cavanaugh dug out a place behind his dead horse for cover. The other men dug the best they could in the hard, rocky ground, but no one made much progress. The dead and dying horses made the best protection.

Arrows began to fly through the air. They had broad iron heads for killing man or buffalo. One horse took four arrows, two puncturing its lungs. It wheezed and bleated in agony. The corporal who had been riding the mount for three years crawled over to the animal and mercifully killed it with a shot to the head.

"Trouble upstream," Sergeant Long called from the left side of the little island.

Captain Cavanaugh looked that way. More than a hundred mounted Indians had formed together upstream, many carrying lances with colorful streamers on them. Some wore paint on their faces, chests, and arms. Others had pieces of white man's clothing on. Those with rifles came in front, and those with bows and arrows behind them.

Suddenly there was a deafening whoop, and they headed downstream, galloping on the sand, then at the last minute breaking into the water and coming directly for the point of the small island.

"They want to overrun us and cut us to pieces!" Captain Cavanaugh bellowed. "Cut down the leaders in the front."

The sharpshooters with the Spencer carbines at the point of the island began firing when the hostiles were at a hundred yards. For these marksmen, it was easier than shooting fish in a barrel. Three of the leaders in the "V" went down in a crash of water and spray. The other men commenced firing at will on Cavanaugh's order as the enemy force came closer.

More than a dozen horses and men went down in the center of the charging mass. The warriors were twenty yards from the point of the island before they hesitated, then broke the attack and charged down both sides of the island.

Men along the sides of the small spit of land poured more gunfire into the attackers, and they rushed past and regrouped downstream, well out of range.

"Broke them, by God!" Captain Cavanaugh roared. "Good work, men! They'll come that way again. They've got plenty of manpower."

He looked around the island as men dug frantically with hands and tin plates, even spoons. He asked Lieutenant O'Hara to check for casualties.

"Keep it informal, look around. I don't want the men to know how many we've lost."

Lieutenant O'Hara rolled across a dead horse and crawled along the flat ground to check on the men.

Lieutenant Winchester lay behind his dead mount. He fired randomly now and then with his Spencer, but Cavanaugh didn't have time to worry about him.

"Doing fine, men!" Captain Cavanaugh called so everyone on the island could hear him over the sporadic rifle fire. The snipers on the cliffs wounded two more men.

"Here they come again!" a trooper yelled. Twenty five mounted warriors charged the island, then circled it. Before they'd completed one turn of the island, four of the warriors were dead in the hot sand of the riverbed. They withdrew.

The sniping from the cliff was deadly. One corporal took a round through the chest and died in his friend's arms. By now, every horse on the island was dead or dying. The sun blistered down on them. Water was close by, but an attempt to fill up a canteen brought a flurry of hostile arrows and rifle shots.

A trooper screamed on one side of the island, and Medical Sergeant Foland squirmed through the men to get to his side. He saw that an arrow was in the man's leg beyond the end of the arrowhead. He broke off the shaft with pliers and, before the trooper could protest, hit the broken end of the arrow and drove it on through his thigh until it came out the other side. The trooper fainted. Foland threw the bloody arrow away and tied up the wound, then hurried over to the next wounded man.

Captain Cavanaugh directed four men to leave one side of the island and run to the other to balance the defense, though there was a good chance they'd be hit by sniper gunfire on their way. Miraculously all four made it untouched.

The enemy gunmen were no more than 300 yards away, and their superior vantage point made it impossible for the troopers to devise any solid protection. If the hostiles had been better shots, Cavanaugh knew that his company could have been wiped out in an hour.

"Enemy charge," one of the point men bellowed. Captain Cavanaugh looked upstream. At least three hundred warriors were forming into a single group, their ponies prancing, rifles and bow and arrows at the ready.

"Hold your fire until they get within seventy-five yards," Captain Cavanaugh roared. "Make every shot kill an Indian!"

A small cheer went up, and just then a sudden rain of arrows dropped silently out of the sky. Two troopers called out in pain. Sergeant Foland ran toward the men. He stumbled, and Captain Cavanaugh saw a bright red bloodstain blossom on his pants leg.

"Damn it, Foland's down," he muttered to no one. He rolled across the top of his horse and ran upright for ten yards, then he dove into a small depression behind a horse and looked at the medic a few feet away.

"Hell, Captain, it's just a scratch," Foland called. "I got to get over to Phillips. Looks like that arrow caught him bad." The medic crawled away across the sandy island, past some wild plum brush. He stopped and picked up a ripe plum and chewed on it. "Not bad, Captain," he said, then vanished behind the brush.

Captain Cavanaugh shook his head, then worked his way up toward the front of the little island. He could see the five men lying flat in the tall grass. If the hostiles broke through there and got on that spit of land, they would overrun the whole island and the battle would be over.

"Ready weapons!" he shouted, bringing up his own Spencer. He had laid out two extra tubes of seven rounds each, and he bellied down in the sand where he could fire over the heads of the five men at the point.

The Indians, some Cheyenne, some Sioux, charged the point again. This time they splashed through the water directly at the tip of the island. The splashing of the hooves in the shallow water sent up a spray that formed a kind of screen.

"Fire at will!" Cavanaugh shouted and began shooting himself when the enemy got within range. The troopers' rounds began to take effect. Captain Cavanaugh fired at the lead man, missed, fired again, and saw him tumble off his mount. He lowered his sights and fired at the horses.

He took two of the mounts down, making others behind stumble over them or swing around. He reloaded a tube of rounds and cracked out seven more shots, blasting two more Sioux from their mounts and cutting down two more Indian ponies, sending their riders into the water, in the way of the riders behind them.

As the hostiles pounded closer through the shallow water, the fire from the Spencers and carbines on the island came as a lead wall. Dozens of the Indians fell, and half as many horses went down. Twenty yards from the point of the island, the attackers broke like before and raced along each side. The men along these areas laid down more firepower into the hostiles.

Captain Cavanaugh was just about ready to move back toward his command post in the middle of the island when a searing, white hot pain daggered through his left thigh. He groaned and twisted to one side. A Sioux arrow had penetrated his leg. He gritted his teeth at the terrible pain. Reaching down, he held the arrow in both hands, then with a surge of energy he broke the arrow shaft in half. He roared in pain.

A moment later, Sergeant Foland rolled over next to him.

"Join the walking wounded, Captain. Good work on that arrow. Most men can't do that themselves. I'll carry your Spencer if you want to get back to your hole."

They made it several minutes later. Twice Captain Cavanaugh had to pause and let his head clear from the pain. He slumped in his shallow hole behind the dead horse and stared at Foland.

"I'm fine, Sergeant. Tend to the wounded," he said calmly.

"I am, sir." Foland wrapped a bandage around the captain's leg to stop any bleeding around the shaft, then rolled away and headed for another man who had been hit by a sniper from the cliffs.

Lieutenant O'Hara looked over the dead horse at his commander.

"Sorry you got hit, sir. I'll do the roadwork for you."

"Just keep shooting the bastards," Cavanaugh said. "What time is it?"

Lieutenant O'Hara looked at his pocket watch. "Not quite ten A.M., sir."

"Christ, feels like six in the evening. They don't like our firepower, do they? We got to get every man in the company a repeating rifle. Blew hell out of those charges. Don't think the hostiles have ever gone up against half a company with Spencers before."

Another rain of broad-tipped arrows fell from the sky. This time they all missed human flesh.

"You thinking about tonight, sir?" O'Hara asked.

"Yep. Who are your two best men?"

"Captain, what about our scouts? We could send them."

"Like to, but one is dead and another one wounded in the leg. Eagle Feather has a hurt hand. I'm not sure that he wants to walk eighty-five miles back to the fort."

"I'll think on it, Captain. First they'll have to get through the Indians out there. They'll be waiting for us to send somebody out."

"Where's Winchester gone?"

O'Hara looked over his shoulder. "He's not functioning, Captain. Just huddles there. He's not wounded. I tried to talk to him. He just says, 'So many die, so many die.'"

"My fault, Lieutenant O'Hara. I should have figured it out and left him at the fort."

"Enemy charge!" a voice called from the point. They looked upriver. This time there were fewer Indians, no more than two hundred, Cavanaugh guessed.

"Load a new tube in your Spencers and leave a round in the chamber," Cavanaugh bellowed. "Let's knock the bastards down again."

He waited as the men reloaded. "No one fires until they get to within fifty yards of the point," the captain called.

As they waited for the charging Indians to get within range, Captain Cavanaugh looked upstream along the shore and saw a sudden surge of movement — mounted warriors he didn't think had even been in the battle yet. It was as if a new spirit moved the warriors. Then he looked back at the hostiles charging. When they were at fifty yards he brayed out the command, "Fire!"

The first volley from the carbines on the island slammed into the front riders like a steel scythe, cutting down warriors and horses in a massive wave. The horses behind the leaders stumbled and some fell. Others had to jump over fallen comrades, and when they did, the second volley smashed into them.

On the third volley the Indians were only thirty yards away from the point of the island. More horses and warriors fell. The fifth and sixth rounds splattered into the struggling horses and Indians, and as it did, the ranks split once more and the warriors surged around the island.

The weary troopers cheered. Rifle fire from the cliffs increased as the mass attacks began. Two more men were hit and then Captain Cavanaugh took his second wound, a chunk of forearm flesh taken by a stray bullet. Cursing loudly, he wrapped up his arm with his kerchief. He was about to pass out again, then came to by pure willpower and looked around. He checked his field. There was no sense in asking for a casualty report. Before this was over they would all be casualties in one way or another.

Chapter Fourteen

There were no more mass attacks the rest of the afternoon. The hostiles kept shooting arrows onto the island, and the riflemen on the cliffs maintained their fire, pinning the troopers in whatever cover they had found.

Five more times a combined force of fifty or sixty Sioux, Arapaho, and Cheyenne charged directly at the island from one side or the other, then while still fifty yards away, fired and splayed off in both directions, breaking off the attack.

At the first hint of darkness, O'Hara came up to Captain Cavanaugh's pit with two men. One was Private Holder, the youngest man in the company. The other was a corporal who had six years service.

"You know what we want you men to do?" Captain Cavanaugh asked the two troopers.

"Yes, sir," Holder said. "We sneak past these red-skin heathens and hike due southeast until we get to Fort Wallace, or find some transportation to get us there faster. We send back a rescue column."

"Right. It might be better if you go separate routes. Then if the Indians catch one of you, the other might still get through. We're counting on you men. Otherwise, all of us here are dead."

"Yes, sir," Holder said. "We best get moving. Give us more time before daylight. We got to be hell and gone from this valley by then to get clear of them injuns."

Captain Cavanaugh nodded and waved them off. They had their pistols, knives, and double canteens, plus a five-pound slab of horse meat apiece which they could cook once they got far enough away to be safe. The last Cavanaugh saw of them, they had left the upstream tip of the island. That was the direction away from most of the savages.

The men had planned on walking quietly up the shallow watercourse as far as they could so they wouldn't leave any tracks. When they left the stream they would walk backward without their boots on so it would look like someone entering the stream.

Captain Cavanaugh said a quick prayer for their safe journey, then asked Lieutenant O'Hara to check casualties. Cavanaugh couldn't move. His thigh had stopped bleeding but throbbed with pain. The arrow in his thigh would have to come out long before any relief party might arrive.

He didn't like to think about how long they would have to hold out on the island. One day was already gone. If the scouts could get past the Indians, it would take them at least four days to walk the eighty-five miles to Wallace, then another two or three days for the first elements of a relief column to reach them. At least six more days!

The troopers here couldn't eat the salt pork they brought. It was useless unless they could cook it, and no fires were possible; they would become instant targets. In the darkness he heard men drinking and filling canteens at the water. Some of the troopers cut fresh meat off the dead horses and tried to eat it raw, but even the strongest stomach could barely hold it down.

An unwounded trooper came at Captain Cavanaugh's request, found the officer's horse, and brought his saddlebags. He'd had to cut them in half to get them off the dead animal.

The captain took out a kit of shaving gear and his canteen. He gave out most of the hardtack he found in his saddlebags, and the long, hard strips of jerky. He put the straight razor in his shirt pocket along with a small flask of whiskey.

Lieutenant O'Hara came back with his report.

"Sir, we have fourteen wounded; there are five dead. Lieutenant Winchester is about the same. He huddles behind his dead horse talking to himself. I thought of tying him up so he wouldn't hurt himself, but I don't believe that's necessary."

"I see. Are you wounded, O'Hara?"

"No, sir, at least, not yet. I've put four men on guard, one on each side and end of the island. Don't think we'll need them, but in this situation . . . "

"Good idea." Cavanaugh gritted his teeth in pain. "Lieutenant, I am turning command over to you for the duration of this battle. Inform the men." O'Hara saluted and turned to go. "And I'll stand guard on one shift. Tell me when. I'm not doing anything except sitting here, anyway."

There hadn't been a shot fired for two hours. The calm was unreal after being under attack all day. He knew the Indians were afraid to fight after dark. They believed that if they died in the dark, their spirits would become lost and never find their way into their version of heaven.

Cavanaugh used some water in his mess cup and his shaving brush and shaved as best he could without a mirror. He washed his face, head, neck, then had a man fill his canteen again. He tried to think of some way to store water for use the next day when it got so hot, but there were no available containers. After his turn at watch, he managed to get some sleep.

Lieutenant O'Hara had rifled every saddlebag on the island and brought out all of the ammunition they had, distributing it among the men. They had enough for another two or three days of good fighting, then they'd have to be careful how often they shot.

As the sun lighted the eastern sky, he saw the hostiles gathering upstream and on the right-hand riverbank, where most had been assembled before. Now there seemed to be a new enthusiasm for the fight. He wished he knew what it was all about.

Silver Bear had ridden into the clearing near the twin cottonwoods where the three tribes had been gathering for the day's fight. A murmur went through the three or four hundred Indian braves. All had heard that Silver Bear had been in their camp for two days, but that he would not lead their fight. He had violated one of his sacred taboos the night before the first fight with the white eyes.

There had not been time for his purification. It took three days of rituals and intense concentration to cleanse him so the magic of his war bonnet would keep him safe and bring his people to victory over the pony soldiers. He had told his people that if he fought without his strong magic, he would surely die and the people would suffer defeat.

He sat in a small tepee near the river all day and heard reports of how the warriors had been thrown back time and time again by the small number of white eyes. He bowed his head in pain and anger but knew he could do nothing.

Then Running Free had pushed into the small tepee and shook his head. Running Free was a Cheyenne and proud of his tribe. He was angry at Silver Bear.

"You are showing the Sioux and Arapaho that you and the rest of the Cheyenne are cowards. How can you sit on your lance when your people, your family, are being shot down by the white eyes?

"I have taken one of the white-eye bullets, but I still ride on the attack. Are you a coward, Silver Bear?"

Silver Bear waved him away, but a few minutes later he rose from where he sat, said an incantation to the gods, then put on his war bonnet, took his heavy Sharps rifle, and called for his war pony.

A wave of joy swept before him as he rode from the war camp toward the river. Two hundred warriors fell in behind him. By the time he got to the river, word had spread that Silver Bear had come and would lead the charge. Silver Bear would save the day and they would overwhelm the white-eye Horse Soldiers. Every warrior must be ready to take many scalps and count dozens of coups.

The Cheyenne warrior chief sat on his large white stallion and stared at the small island where the white eyes huddled. "They are like mice in their puny dens just under the sod. We will rout them and kill every one of them on the island."

He looked around and saw Sioux and Arapaho and his own Cheyenne brothers. He lifted his lance. "It is time we finish this. Follow me, and we will run the white eye through a dozen times and take his scalp and his long guns. Today we will fight with bravery and win a great victory! It will be the first to come from our gathering together!"

His very appearance and his willingness to fight galvanized the Indians into action. Silver Bear took the point in the arrowhead Indian attack formation. Cheyenne, Arapaho, and Sioux mixed in the boiling sea of warriors behind the great leader. They spread out, and soon there were over 600 warriors moving forward. When they were three hundred yards from the point of the island, Silver Bear lifted his heavy white-eye rifle and bellowed out a Cheyenne war cry.

The six hundred behind him screamed their own battle cries, and the massive wave of warriors swept forward. Nothing could stop it.

Every man on the island saw the attack begin. They didn't need to be told to load a full tube of rounds into the Spencers and lay out rows of ammunition for the Sharps carbines.

"We fire at seventy-five yards," Lieutenant O'Hara ordered. His voice was becoming hoarse. He looked at Captain Cavanaugh as he readied his own rifles.

"How many of the wounded can fire their weapons?" Captain Cavanaugh asked calmly as he saw the 600 painted, screaming warriors bearing down on them.

"All but two, sir," Lieutenant O'Hara said. "They're holding up remarkably well."

"So are you, O'Hara. How is that arrow wound in your arm from the other patrol?"

"I don't think about it, sir. I pretend it isn't there."

"Damned well wish I could do the same. Christ, I wish I could walk!"

"Later, sir. We'll get you patched up."

"Take a surgeon to — "

"Hostiles at one-hundred yards." Lieutenant O'Hara bent down behind a dead horse and lifted his Spencer carbine. "No sense in firing in volleys," he bellowed. "Each man fire at will after they're within seventy-five yards. Don't waste a round. Eight rounds, eight dead savages. Let's get ready."

The hostiles began firing from the front row when they were a hundred yards away. A trooper on the left side of the island wailed in pain as he was hit in the side. He slumped over his carbine, then rose, wiped away the blood, and prepared to fire.

"Now!" Lieutenant O'Hara bellowed.

The Sharps barked, fresh rounds slammed into the breach and fired again. The Spencers roared one after another. A dozen horses went down. Four warriors fell off their mounts into the jumble of trampling hooves behind them.

The firing came in surges, as the men needed so many seconds to reload. The second spate of firing dropped another six or eight horses and riders, but Silver Bear on his huge white stallion swept forward untouched through the bullets thick as raindrops in a thunderstorm.

After the third heavy firing, the Indians on the outer wings began to close in. Now they came under heavier fire and half a dozen stumbled and sent riders into the sand or water.

The spray from the horses in the shallow stream was like a silver curtain for the Indians. It hid some of them but did not deflect bullets.

The fifth round of shots from the Spencers blasted a hole in the men around Silver Bear, but still he charged forward. He came ahead of the others and angled for the very point of the spit of land. Four of the five troopers out there with Spencers lifted their aim as the big horse thundered almost to dry land. They all fired together and horse and rider faltered.

Silver Bear held his seat for a second, then slammed off the left side of his large mount and splashed into the water, twenty feet from the shore. His big stallion took another step, then crumpled into the water just beyond Silver Bear.

The warriors riding behind him couldn't believe it. Many stopped firing when they saw their leader fall. Some on the ends of the line turned and rode away. The rest, pushed by the riders behind, broke around the island in two big rivers of warriors, too shocked to go on firing. They stared at their fallen leader, Silver Bear, the great man who could not be hurt by white-eye bullets.

Now he lay dead in the water near his magnificent dead war pony. On the island, the troopers watched the warriors stream by. "That took all the fight out of them!" one jubilant sergeant cried as he fired the last round in his Spencer and reached for a full tube.

Captain Cavanaugh lay sprawled in his hole behind the horse. Blood snaked down the side of his head.

"We did it again, Captain," Lieutenant O'Hara said. When he got no response, he crawled over to the captain, saw his wound, and swore. At once he rose up in the line of fire and scooted across the dead horse to drop in beside the captain. He checked the head wound.

The frown on his face eased.

"Captain," O'Hara called. He shook his shoulders slightly. "Captain Cavanaugh!" he said louder. Eyelids fluttered, then came open.

"Christ, who kicked me in the head?"

"An Indian's bullet, sir. Creased your skull and knocked you out. As long as you can talk, it can't be too bad."

"Nobody ever stopped me from talking."

O'Hara wiped the blood off, then washed the wound with some water from his canteen and called for Sergeant Foland.

The sergeant dragged himself into the hole and O'Hara heaved out of it. Two rifle bullets jolted into the horse, as if some redskin had been waiting for him to move.

"Not much damage here, sir," Foland said. "I'll put a bandage around your head to keep that spot covered. About the only way I can do it."

Eagle Feather worked up toward the captain.

"Hardest charge I ever saw," the head scout said. "Six hundred of them! They all done hard fighting. Great leader dead."

Captain Cavanaugh grinned through his pain. "I think he's right, O'Hara. Never seen anything like that charge. They'll bother us, keep us pinned down, starve us out maybe, but they won't try to run us off here with any real power to it. Putting down the big chief leading that last charge seemed to do it."

As they spoke, fifty Sioux left the main group upstream and charged down toward the island. They were still 200 yards away when a soldier stood up, waved his Spencer carbine and shouted.

"Charge, men! Follow me. We'll get the bastards!" It was Lieutenant Winchester. He took a dozen steps and was beyond the last trooper, striding into the water. "Come on, men, we'll wipe out this little bunch and go back to the fort for a hot supper!" He lurched then as a rifle bullet hit him from the cliff.

"Winchester! Get back here!" Captain Cavanaugh's voice blasted out at the officer.

The crazed lieutenant lifted his carbine and fired into empty space. Another rifle round hit him, driving him back a step. Then four more rounds caught the easy target. He half turned, dropped to one knee, then a round hit him in the side of the head and smashed him sideways into the water. He lay there without moving, his face under water.

"My God!" Lieutenant O'Hara exclaimed.

"Stand in your positions!" Captain Cavanaugh shouted. "No man is to retrieve the lieutenant's body until dark. He died in the line of duty. Now let's keep alert and stay down if you want to stay alive!"

O'Hara looked over the dead horse at his captain. "Sir, I . . ."

"We'll sort it out later. Right now, we stay alive."

"Yes, sir." He paused. "Captain, you hear any shooting last night? The two scouts. You think they made it through the Indians?"

"Might have. I didn't hear anything. If they did, we're still looking at five days before reinforcements arrive."

There were two more charges that day, but not more than a hundred warriors on either. The first was shattered so badly the Indians never got nearer than fifty yards to the island. In the last one, the warriors gave up before they even reached the water.

What hurt the most was the rifle fire from the cliffs. Now the men on the island could return some fire at the cliffs and it reduced the enemy shots for a while.

The hot sun was out again with not a cloud to mar the beautiful blue sky . . . only now it was a curse. Some of the wounded called for water. Most could move about a bit and toss canteens from one to another.

Captain Cavanaugh shook his head. For just a moment he saw two of everything. He had lost too much blood and had had nothing to eat for a day and a half beside hardtack. It tasted like sawdust. Salt pork would taste good. They had to figure out how to get some fires going so that the Sioux couldn't see.

He moved and yelped in pain. His damn leg. That arrow had to come out. Maybe now Sergeant Foland would do it. The redness around the arrow shaft had burned black. His left thigh was swelling. He could get blood poisoning and die by daybreak.

Chapter Fifteen

Sergeant Foland crawled around the horse, dragging the leg that had been shot. Captain Cavanaugh saw the pain on the sergeant's face.

"Foland, have you taken time to wrap up that leg of yours?"

He looked up, surprised at the question. "Yes, sir, last night. Hurts a mite, but I'll be fine."

"Maybe so, maybe not. You ever cut an arrowhead out of a leg?"

Foland hooded his eyes, his face tight. "No, sir. Can it be driven on through?"

"I don't know."

Foland looked at the tear in the captain's pants leg where the jagged end of the arrow shaft protruded.

"Flesh is going bad around the wound. You're right, sir, it can't wait five or six more days. But I don't have a proper cutting scalpel for this."

"I do. Sharp as any sawbones' knife." Captain Cavanaugh handed him the straight razor.

Foland shook his head. "Don't rightly think so, sir. Never cut that much before. Rather not start on you."

"Sergeant, look at the wound. That iron can stay in my leg another day at the most, then it does its work and I've got blood poisoning. You know about that, right?"

"Yes, sir."

"I'd be dead a day later. Either the arrowhead comes out or you cut off my leg."

"I'm not a surgeon, sir. I respectfully tell you that Dr. Lassiter told me not to do any cutting like this. Said I'd botch the job and kill somebody. He ordered me not to cut. He's a major, sir.

"I know he's — " Marcus Cavanaugh looked away. The rate of fire coming from the cliffs had slackened off. He could tell there were not nearly as many hostiles around the twin cottonwoods as before. The warriors were starting to drift off. "Sergeant, could you get something to soak up some blood so I can see what I'm doing. I'll cut the damn iron out myself. You stand by to help me. Can you do that?"

"Yes, sir."

The enlisted medic dug in his shoulder bag and came out with a square of white cloth.

"It's clean, sir. I've been saving it."

He huddled near the commander, who held the open straight edge razor.

"I . . . I might not be speaking plainly after I start to cut. What I intend to do is to cut down a little wider than the slice the arrowhead made. You spread back the muscle and flesh and mop up the blood. When I get the outer prongs of the arrowhead free, you yank that shaft with all your might and pull it out of there. Understand?"

"Yes, sir." The sergeant looked up. "Sir, do you want somebody to hold your leg still?"

"I'll hold it still, Sergeant."

"But . . ."

"Think about it, Sergeant. It's like a beaver that gets caught in a trap and chews off its own foot. I either go in and get that iron out of me — or I die where I lie, and damn soon. Let's get started."

Lieutenant O'Hara had heard most of it. He pushed up and lay on the other side of the captain.

"I might be able to help," he said. "Put your kerchief in your mouth, sir, so's you won't bite off your tongue."

Captain Cavanaugh nodded at him, stuffed the material into his mouth, then squinted slightly as he lay the straight razor on the end of the gash on his upper thigh. He took a deep breath, then gasped as he forced the razor into the wound the arrowhead had made and sliced it a half-inch wider on each end. A low strangled moan seeped out of the gag. Sweat popped out on his forehead. His eyes went wide, then he let out a long breath through his nose.

Sergeant Foland gripped the sides of the cut and forced the flesh apart. Lieutenant O'Hara did the same on the other half of the wound. Blood rose like a spring, soaking the white cloth in Foland's hand. The captain used the razor again, slicing deeper in the flesh along the wider line. Captain Cavanaugh shivered uncontrollably for a moment. He let go of the razor handle and Sergeant Foland caught it.

The captain took a long breath, his nostrils flaring, then took the razor and finished the slice on the three-inch-long cut. Blood surged again. Sergeant Foland soaked it up and let O'Hara hold the flesh apart.

"The arrowhead point missed the bone, sir," Foland said.

Sweat ran down Captain Cavanaugh's face and into his eyes. Sergeant Foland had been watching. He patted the captain's face with his sleeve.

"I'm gonna try the shaft," Foland said. Cavanaugh nodded.

The medic touched the shaft that extended five inches out of the leg. He closed his fingers around it carefully without any sudden movement, then gave a sudden pull upward. His hand slid off the thin willow stick.

Captain Cavanaugh grunted with pain. He shook his head, spit out the gag, and moaned terribly.

The blood came again, more this time. It flowed out of the trough and down Cavanaugh's leg. Foland tried to sponge up the blood but the entire cloth was saturated. He folded it and wrung it out on the ground, then soaked up more blood from the open wound. The moment he moved the cloth, Cavanaugh pushed down the razor and cut again.

He screamed. As soon as the razor came out, Sergeant Foland had grasped the shaft again. This time he pulled slowly, but steadily. The shaft moved up an inch.

Captain Cavanaugh stiffened. His face and shoulders shook with the terrible pain. He looked away, his head trembling hard, his eyes now closed tightly.

"Pull, you sonofabitch!" Cavanaugh shouted.

Blood flowed over the wound now. Sergeant Foland wiped the small arrow shaft free of blood, closed his hand around it, and then his other hand around the first, and pulled slowly again. Suddenly he jerked upward with his whole torso and arms. The bloody arrow point jolted out, its back wings tearing flesh on its way.

Captain Marcus Cavanaugh saw it, then bellowed in pain and victory as he doubled over in agony. He let out another terrible roar of anger and mind-smashing pain. Then he fainted. The medic lay him back in his shallow hole, took out a heavy compress and pushed it on the wound, then bandaged and wrapped the leg again. He put on another compress and wrapped it with a dozen more windings of what looked like officer's sheets torn into strips.

"Never saw a man take pain like that," Foland said as he stepped over the unconscious officer to wash his hands in the river.

"Ain't many men like our Captain Cavanaugh in this man's army," Lieutenant O'Hara responded, still trembling from the ordeal. "Now get along to tend to the other wounded and — "

Suddenly, two rifle rounds came in from the cliff and one of them hit the horse protecting Captain Cavanaugh.

"Let's spread it out, Sergeant. We're too good a target bunched up this way. Take it easy on your leg. We don't want to lose you."

"Couldn't blast me out of here with a whole keg of black powder, Lieutenant."

The day wore out and soon dusk came. The hostiles on the cliffs had fired only a dozen times all afternoon and there had been no new flights of arrows at all.

Most of the men had begun eating the salt pork. They let it heat in the sun in their big cups. It barely got warm and tasted like lard going down. The hardtack was gone. Raw horse meat was starting to putrefy, but still some men ate it. Half the troop who could eat had violent stomach cramps and vomiting. They cleaned out and drank as much water as they could hold as soon as it was dark.

"A man can live nine days on water alone," somebody said, and the story shot around the camp. Lieutenant O'Hara found Captain Cavanaugh still asleep when he checked back. He let him sleep the night through.

They posted guards, but there was little need. There had been two or three hundred campfires the night before along both sides of the wide riverbed. Now they could see less than six, all on the right hand side looking downstream.

"Most of them are leaving," O'Hara told the men. He went to the water's edge, bent over, and waded out silently in the ankle-deep blackness until he found Lieutenant Winchester. He dragged him back to the shore.

"Don't want some savage to claim his body tonight and desecrate it," he told the medic.

Morning came, clear and warm. The chill of the night air was soon replaced with a warm September sun. Captain Cavanaugh sat up and stared at the cliffs. He hadn't heard a single shot since the sun came up.

As the thought occurred to him, four rifle bullets slapped into the island. So the hostile snipers were still there. The bastards were leaving a rear guard to

170

keep them pinned down and starve them out. Then, with everyone on the island too weak to lift a Spencer, two warriors could sweep in and finish off the survivors and claim all the weapons.

Damn sneaky.

Did Holder and his friend get through the Indians? The two men heading for Fort Wallace had been gone two nights and one day. Cavanaugh wondered how far they had traveled, or if they were even alive. This was the third day of the siege. Now it was a matter of survival. Eagle Feather found a spot where he figured was protected from the cliff riflemen. He made a small fire from dry wood, but now there was little food left. The salt pork had turned rancid and had to be boiled, then fried, to make it edible.

Within minutes after starting the fire, three shots came slamming through the brush, nearly hitting Eagle Feather and he gave up the idea. There was really nothing to cook anyway.

Virtually every trooper on the island was wounded. One man had broken his leg diving into a hole, once when the arrows had come. He'd made a splint for it himself out of plum wood branches. Five sticks each about an inch thick were placed around his lower leg and tied securely with strips of cloth.

On the fourth day, the wails from some of the wounded came more often. Foland had few supplies left to help them. They needed proper medical attention and food.

A coyote wandered onto the island and was shot and skinned. Eagle Feather worked up another fire, and this time it escaped detection. He fried the coyote and each man got a small portion. It was little more than an appetizer, but it perked up the men's spirits some.

As the sun went down on the fourth day, they could see no warrior fires. Only a few calls came from the cliffs from one side to the other.

There never had been any thought on the captain's part of walking out of the fortress they had made of the small island. On foot and away from what protection they had on the island, his tiny force could be run down and slaughtered by only ten or twenty warriors.

Private Fred Holder sat up under some brush near a creek and looked at the sun. It was three hours since he lay down to rest. Enough. He drank his fill at the stream, topped off his canteens with fresh water, and struck out southeast toward Fort Wallace.

He had been on the way for almost three full days and was coming up to the fourth night. He hadn't seen Kincaid since they split up as they left the stream back in the Arikaree valley. Holder had pushed himself, walking twenty hours a day and allowing himself four hours to sleep. An hour later, crossing the hot grasslands, he shook his head and closed his eyes. He was seeing double. He took a drink of water and kept his eyes closed for a minute. When he opened them his vision was normal again. The next river he crossed had to be the southern branch of the Smoky Hill. All he had to do was follow it downstream to Fort Wallace.

That night he shot a jackrabbit and ate until he couldn't swallow another morsel. He slept and when he woke, ate the rest of the roasted rabbit before heading off again, hoping that would be enough to last him to the fort.

The sun was an hour from going down when he saw what he thought was another brush line ahead. A river? Or just a small creek feeding into the Smoky Hill? He wasn't sure. His eyes filmed over and he wiped them, but still he couldn't see clearly. He stopped and gently splashed his face with water from his canteen.

Trudging slowly, wavering now and then, he saw buildings in the distance. He walked forward but found he was veering to the left in a slow arc. He stopped and stared at the buildings. Was it a farm? Or was that the officers' quarters?

Holder figured he was within a quarter mile of whatever it was. Then he stumbled and fell. It took all his strength to stand. When he finally did, he was facing the wrong direction. Three precious steps later he realized it and turned slowly. He took another dozen steps before he stumbled and dropped to his knees, then slowly fell on his shoulder and rolled to his back.

It took Private Holder five minutes to sit up. His eyes misted over again. He pulled out his revolver and pointed it into the air and fired three times, then bent forward and slid to the ground. He was tired, so damn tired, he thought he could sleep right there in the grass for a week.

Chapter Sixteen

The fifth day of the siege, Captain Cavanaugh woke up screaming. His leg was on fire. He had a fever. When the captain controlled his agony, he realized something was different about the valley. Birds were singing. No shots came from the cliffs.

Sergeant Foland crawled up, his leg dragging. He looked at the bandage on the captain's leg and relieved some of the pressure.

"That should make the leg more comfortable."

"Thanks, Sergeant. Not one hell of a lot we can do about it right now. Other times, we hold our lives in our own hands, but not this time. We're depending on the two men we sent out. Either they made it or they didn't."

Lieutenant O'Hara joined the two men and looked at the cliffs. "Sir, I haven't heard a single shot so far since daylight, have you?"

"I think the hostiles have given up and left the area."

"We must have discouraged them a little in their group effort," Lieutenant O'Hara continued. "I mean, if eight hundred of them couldn't even whip forty-eight cavalrymen, what hope do they have?"

"Not a snowball's chance in hell."

It wasn't until that afternoon that the men of Able Troop fully realized that the Indians had left. The hostiles had removed all of their dead during the previous nights. Men began to sit up, and then stand and wander around the island.

"We should bury our dead," Captain Cavanaugh said. "But I know we don't have any tools. We'll wait. Take a good count, O'Hara. I want to know casualties, and how many men with no wounds at all."

There was plenty of time to get the count. Lieutenant O'Hara walked from area to area, making marks on a small pad he carried in his shirt pocket. When he came back, he brought the captain a canteen of fresh water.

"Captain, sir, we have fourteen dead, two seriously wounded who can't last more than another day. We have six wounded who can't walk, and we have fifteen walking wounded. We have a seventy-seven percent casualty rate."

"Damn. Even with the hostiles gone, we can't march out."

"I could take three men and head for the fort. Once we get away from here we're sure to find some game."

"Don't even think about trying it. But game is an idea. Send Eagle Feather and that other Crow out to bring back some game. Now we can have a fire and cook something. The horses are too far gone, but fresh game! Get them moving. Yes, they can use their carbines to hunt."

In the next few hours, Lieutenant O'Hara organized the island into four sections. Each section had two men who were not wounded to take care of those not able to move or who needed help. They cut plum branches and made shade for two men and the captain. Late that afternoon, Eagle Feather and the other scout brought back six jackrabbits.

Most of the game in the area had been frightened away by the gunfire, but jackrabbits seldom tend to wander more than a hundred yards from their home place, even when chased by a coyote. It means they run in circles and are easier to catch.

The big jackrabbits yielded plenty of meat for the men. The rabbits were cut up, and those who could cooked for themselves. No man went without.

After five days in the hot sun, the horses' dead bodies had begun to stink. The men that could walk moved off the island as often as they could to avoid the stench. Some sat with their feet in the cool water during the day, and some of the unwounded splashed in the water and washed the week's grime off their bodies, using sand as soap.

The sixth day passed with still no sign of a rescue party. Eagle Feather had to go out hunting with one of the soldiers because the other Crow scout's arm wound had turned sour. The hunters returned with only two rabbits and one pheasant.

Captain Cavanaugh's fever grew worse. Foland was by his side constantly now. He wet a blouse from one of the dead men and used it to sponge off the captain's face and chest. His leg had swollen again. Twice the captain screamed out in delirium. Lieutenant O'Hara had temporary command of the troups until further notice.

On the seventh day, Eagle Feather came back limping. He had not found any game. Two more of the wounded died, bringing the death count up to sixteen.

"If we don't get help within two days, the captain isn't going to make it," Sergeant Foland told Lieutenant O'Hara.

"He'll make it, Sergeant. He hasn't lived this long to die a day before the relief column gets here."

"Sir, there's at least a fifty-fifty chance those men didn't even get through the Indians. They both might be hanging over some Cheyenne roasting fire head down right now."

"I can't believe that, Foland. But if I want to maintain control of myself, I can't dwell on it. You and I still have thirty-two lives in our hands. Let's not lose any more of them."

Eagle Feather could not hunt on the eighth day. Lieutenant O'Hara sent two privates out instead. Both had been hunters in Tennessee. They came back at noon with four squirrels, a pheasant, and a jackrabbit. The men ate everything but the fur and bones.

Captain Cavanaugh threw off the fever for a while. He approved of what O'Hara had done, but two hours later he slipped back into the high fever and wandered in and out of consciousness.

A light sprinkle of rain ushered in the ninth day before the wind blew away the dark clouds and left fluffy balls of cotton high in the sky, and a bright, warm sun that dried off the valley. Eagle Feather's leg was better, so he took the two hunters from the day before and went in search of game.

Later that morning, Lieutenant O'Hara saw movement from the ridge of hills to the southeast.

"Look alive, men!" he bellowed. "Riders to the south and east on the ridge."

They all strained to see, but all they could make out were figures on horseback.

"Build a fire!" Lieutenant O'Hara roared. He helped, and they put green plum branches on top to make smoke. "The Indians know where we are already," the officer said. "If that's a friendly force, we want to be sure they can see us."

The fire blazed up and a smoke column went skyward. A moment later they heard the sterling notes of an army trumpeter blowing the charge call.

Tears streamed down Lieutenant O'Hara's face. Some of the men ran into the shallow water toward the stream of horsemen that worked down the slope and raced along the river toward them.

Captain Cavanaugh rose and stared at the men. "Lieutenant, what is going on? Maintain some discipline with these troops."

"Captain, they're here. A relief column is coming downstream. We heard a bugle call. They should be here soon." Captain Cavanaugh blinked back tears, then let them come. He rubbed them away and pushed back the shelter the men had made for him to keep the sun away.

A few of the men without wounds had splashed across the river and waited on the other side. Their enthusiasm gave them a surge of energy that soon waned. Some of them dropped to their knees to wait.

The first mounted trooper to break through the screen of brush from upstream and splash across the stream looked familiar.

"It's Private Holder!" Captain Cavanaugh shouted. "He made it, the boy got through."

Holder stopped on the sandy shore on the island in front of a crowd of cheering men and tore open his saddlebags, pulling out strips of jerky and hardtack and some smashed loaves of bread. The hard bread had touches of blue mold on it, but nobody minded. They ate, chewed on the jerky, and pounded Holder on the back until he nearly fell.

He walked over to where Captain Cavanaugh lay.

"Sir, Private Holder reporting. My assignment is completed. A relief party is arriving. Three ambulances and a supply wagon are a day behind us, but we have two pack mules with enough food for half an army."

Captain Cavanaugh reached out for the trooper and hugged him. Both men were crying. Holder brought out a chocolate bar that had melted at least once and hardened again.

"This is to keep up your strength, sir. Major Owensby himself is leading the column, and Dr. Lassiter is in the ambulance."

"Thank you, *Corporal* Holder," Captain Cavanaugh said. "You just earned yourself a promotion."

Then Holder was swept away by the men, who pounded him on the back and asked all sorts of questions.

He returned a minute later. "Sir, I'm sorry, but I don't think Wilson got through. He didn't get to the fort and we couldn't find him on the way back. I almost didn't make it myself. I passed out near a little ranch ten miles from the fort. Luckily, them folks heard my shots and took me in. They helped me get to the fort."

"Good work, Corporal Holder," Lieutenant O'Hara said. "As you were."

By the time Major Owensby arrived that evening, the thirty-two survivors were all sitting down eating rations and special food the troopers had brought them. The major stared at Captain Cavanaugh and shook his head. "Looks like you stopped half the lead and arrows the hostiles threw."

"Some of it, sir."

The major looked around. He saw thirty-five dead horses on the island, and another thirty or forty near the point of the island and along both sides.

"Seems like you men were busy. You rest easy, Cavanaugh. Dr. Lassiter is coming across the stream now with his black bag and ambulance rig. He'll have you feeling better in no time." He grimaced. "Damn, those horses stink."

"Yes, sir."

"Oh, we ran across one poor wretch on the way here. Looked like he was a prospector, but one of the men said he was the Indian trader from town. Gent said his name was Toby Gates. We run off some Cheyenne, but not before they had tortured the poor devil almost to death.

"Close-mouthed guy, thin as a rifle barrel. The man knew he was dying. Said he wanted to confess. Said he killed the rancher and his wife and girl at the Hedbetter place. We were out there a couple of weeks ago and we agreed it didn't look like Indians. Said he wanted to stir up the Indians by getting Hedbetter's brother to go out and rile them by gunning their camps with a Big Fifty buffalo gun."

"So he caused this whole uprising?" Captain Cavanaugh asked.

"Looks like. He paid the price. He'd lost too much blood — you know how the Cheyenne like to bleed a man. He died and we dug him under. Curious, though, he never said why he did it. But on his horse we found a sack of ore, looks like damn near pure gold to me."

"Keep it quiet," Captain Cavanaugh said. "Just what we don't need up here is a gold rush. We'd have a thousand men stream in here, and the Indians would kill half of them, and then we'd be in a real Indian war."

"My sentiments exactly. I saw it and I had two men bury it before anyone else had a look. Here comes Dr. Lassiter."

Dr. Lassiter worked quickly on Captain Cavanaugh. He brought his fever down, then cleaned his thigh wound with sulphur and stitched and dressed it properly. He shook his head in amazement when Sergeant Foland described how the captain had cut out the arrowhead himself.

The following day the men were ready to leave. The sixteen dead, including Lieutenant Winchester, were buried a good distance off the bank of the Arikaree. There were shovels on the wagons to help dig them out of mires. The bodies were dug in deep and covered with rocks but no markers so the Indians couldn't desecrate them.

No one said a word about how Lieutenant Winchester died, and Major Owensby didn't ask. It would be a small secret the men would never divulge. No reason to shame his family.

A remuda of thirty extra saddled horses had been trailed from the supply wagon. All the Able Troop men fit to ride would be permitted to; the rest would roll along toward the fort in the ambulances and the supply wagon.

A week later, back in Fort Wallace, Captain Cavanaugh was healing well in the sick ward behind Dr. Lassiter's medical office. There were still eight men there from the engagement which had come to be known as the Battle of Cavanaugh's Island.

Major Owensby telegraphed his report on the fight to the Territorial Headquarters in Chicago. He let Lieutenant O'Hara write the majority of it. Within days, the story was on the front page of every newspaper in the country, and Captain Cavanaugh was being hailed as a hero. The details of his cutting an Indian arrowhead out of his thigh grew each time it was reported.

"Some of your supporters around the country," the major said, smiling as he threw down a stack of newspapers next to Cavanaugh's bed. "Hell, don't worry about it. I don't mind that you're more famous than your commanding officer. Besides, I'm mentioned in half of the stories, anyway."

"Seems only fitting, since you sent me on the mission."

The major pulled a sheet of paper out of his jacket and gave it to the captain. "Here. Thought you should know this has gone in. It's a recommendation for a medal for you. Lieutenant O'Hara wrote it up before I even saw it. Recommends you for the Congressional Medal of Honor for bravery and leadership far above and beyond the call of duty in the face of overwhelming enemy odds in the heat of battle. I wrote an endorsement of the letter and sent it to Chicago four or five days ago. Also put in a strong written request that you be promoted to major on merit, before your time in rank is satisfied.

The Army doesn't do it very often these days. Sort of like a field promotion under fire. But I got me a feeling Sheridan will ram it through congress. Now, you got anything to say in your defense?"

Both men chuckled, then Captain Cavanaugh caught the major's hand and shook it firmly. "Major, I don't know what to say. I'm not much on making speeches."

"You spoke right handily to those 900 savages when they made a mass attack on your forty men."

Marcus Cavanaugh laughed softly. "Major, I'd bet by reveille that number will be up to at least fifteen hundred. Might even go to two thousand." He sobered. "We both know I was just in the right place at the right time. If you'd been there, you would have done the same thing. I'll never know why it was me. But I damn well won't turn down the medal or the promotion, if I get them."

"You'll get them, or I'll blow Phil Sheridan out of his britches."

They shook hands again and the major left the papers with the Army's latest hero.

"Oh," Major Owensby added, turning in the doorway, "I thought you might like to know that according to headquarters, this was the first time that an Army troop has ever faced an overwhelming force with repeating rifles. The idea that a small band can stop even 600 savages with repeating rifles and little protection is going to be a big talking point for the Army brass for years. It's also going to be a big factor in how the hostiles look at the Army and our fighting ability. Cavanaugh, I'd say you just earned yourself a full page in the military history books." Major Owensby waved and slipped out the door.

Newly posted at Fort Bowie, Arizona Territory, Major Marcus Cavanaugh joins forces with the courageous 10th Cavalry's Buffalo Soldiers to fight the Apaches in the . . .

FIGHT AT THUNDERHORSE MESA

30 MILLION COPIES OF HIS NOVELS IN PRINT!

☐	BOLD RIDER	10683-4	$2.95
☐	BOUGHT WITH A GUN	10744-X	$2.95
☐	BOUNTY GUNS	10758-X	$2.95
☐	BRAND OF EMPIRE	10770-9	$2.95
☐	THE BRANDED MAN	10785-7	$2.95
☐	FIRST CLAIM	20455-0	$2.95
☐	HARDCASE	20456-9	$2.95
☐	KING COLT	14686-0	$3.50
☐	THE MAN ON THE BLUE	15255-0	$2.95
☐	RAW LAND	17263-2	$2.95
☐	RIDE THE MAN DOWN	20454-2	$2.95